"Given our…attraction to each other, it would be best for me to be reassigned somewhere else within the company for the duration of my contract."

Damon had considered something similar in the depths of the night. Hearing the same suggestion from her didn't stop the quicksilver flash of pain.

"All right. I can have your office moved, or ensure someone is present at future—"

"Which brings me to the third and final piece of business."

He slanted her a dark look. No one dared to interrupt him. She merely stared back at him, and damn if that didn't stir his blood.

"Yes?"

Some of her bravado slipped. She breathed in deeply, her hands settling on her lap as she laced her fingers together.

A blush stole over her cheeks. The sight of her skin turning pink tugged memories of the previous night to the forefront.

"Spit it out, Evolet," he growled.

"All right."

She looked him dead in the eye and he suddenly had the feeling that the world was about to drop out from under him.

"I want you to be my first lover."

Emmy Grayson wrote her first book at the age of seven about a spooky ghost. Her passion for romance novels began a few years later with the discovery of a worn copy of Kathleen E. Woodiwiss's *A Rose in Winter* buried in her mother's bookshelf. She lives in the Midwest countryside with her husband (who's also her ex-husband), their children and enough animals to start their own zoo.

Books by Emmy Grayson

Harlequin Presents

Cinderella Hired for His Revenge

The Infamous Cabrera Brothers

His Billion-Dollar Takeover Temptation
Proof of Their One Hot Night
A Deal for the Tycoon's Diamonds

The Van Ambrose Royals

A Cinderella for the Prince's Revenge
The Prince's Pregnant Secretary

Visit the Author Profile page
at Harlequin.com.

Emmy Grayson

HIS ASSISTANT'S NEW YORK AWAKENING

HARLEQUIN
PRESENTS

Recycling programs
for this product may
not exist in your area.

ISBN-13: 978-1-335-59300-9

His Assistant's New York Awakening

Harlequin Enterprises ULC
22 Adelaide St. West, 41st Floor
Toronto, Ontario M5H 4E3, Canada
www.Harlequin.com

Printed in U.S.A.

HIS ASSISTANT'S
NEW YORK AWAKENING

For Chad, Emma and Gene.

October souls gone too soon.

CHAPTER ONE

THE MUSIC SLID over Damon Bradford's skin like a lover's caress. He sipped his cocktail, the smooth taste of gin lingering on his tongue. Better to focus on that then the slow, languid heat spreading through his veins as he watched her.

The cellist.

Music had never been an important part of his life. He knew the difference between classical and rock, paid hefty sums for bands and singers to perform at the various functions he hosted throughout the year. But the actual music had always been background noise.

Whereas this...the rich somber notes of her solo rising and falling with perfect precision, the languid tempo encouraging listeners to slow down, to forget the demands of life for a moment...

It was unlike anything he'd ever heard before.

Just like the woman behind the cello was unlike anyone he had ever encountered before.

He would have dismissed her at first glance if she hadn't been playing. Blond hair wound into a tight bun at the base of her neck. Black dress loose about the torso, sleeves down to her elbows, a full skirt draped over her knees as she cradled the cello between her legs.

Nondescript. Plain. Boring.

It had been her fingers that had first caught his eye. Pale, slender and elegant as one hand moved the bow with exactitude, the other sliding up and down the strings with graceful mastery that made his muscles tighten.

Turned on by a damn cello.

He sipped his cocktail, savoring the flavors of gin and lavender as he waited for the cool drink to calm his errant libido.

No such luck. The music had penetrated his body, piercing through his custom-tailored tuxedo and the calm, collected exterior he usually portrayed to the world. His gaze was drawn back up to her face.

Wide lips set into a heart-shaped face, the sharp cut of her chin at odds with her rounded cheeks. *Striking* was the first word that came to mind. Yet she downplayed her appearance with simple clothes and a severe hairstyle. A woman, he decided as he listened to her coax emotion out of every note, who was trying to keep the focus on her music and off herself.

The rest of the orchestra joined in, the harmony of the four dozen or so instruments filling the ballroom. A volunteer symphony made up of musicians still working toward their big breaks. He'd been hesitant when his event manager, Kimberly, had submitted the entertainment schedule and it included the opening-hour music being performed by the New York City Apprentice Symphony. When he'd questioned her, she had presented it as an opportunity to engage with a community organization.

With one more glance at the woman who had captured his attention, he was suddenly very glad he'd let Kimberly have her way.

Damon tore his gaze away from the cellist and gazed out over the modern ballroom, filled with the richest people in New York City.

The majority of the guests at the annual Bradford Global Gala Fundraiser were there to be seen in their most expensive clothes, enjoy exclusive cocktails, perhaps pick up a new lover or cement a business deal over caviar. A couple were there because they genuinely wanted to see a new wing added to the children's hospital, the selected recipient of this year's fundraiser.

But none were there because of the music.

A pity, Damon thought as he watched the crowd of people talking, laughing. Unfortunately, he was more like them than he cared to admit. Not noticing the simple joys around him. Always focused on something else, the next to-do on his never-ending list. He moved from one goal to another with thoroughness and a speed that impressed his employees and clients, irritated his competitors and, most importantly, kept him moving forward.

Never back.

Yet he had found himself at that place he'd heard others mumble and complain about but never thought he himself would end up at—a crossroads. Bradford Global was one of the top manufacturers of a variety of products and was in the final running for a major contract with a luxury European airline. He owned homes on four continents, spoke three languages fluently and was a frequent feature on the covers of magazines like *Fortune*. Edward Charles Damon Bradford had it all.

So why did he feel so damn empty?

It was a notable lack of pleasure, joy, even a hint of contentment that had driven him to the edge of the ballroom tonight. Restlessness had carried his feet past the people trying to get his attention, past his personal assistant and the event coordinator wanting his input on the décor to the secluded alcove. Boredom had driven him to sit down in one of the two wingback chairs hidden from view of most of the people milling about, his primary view the musicians on the elevated stage. He had wanted different, craved a change, no matter how small.

And he'd found that change sitting toward the back wall of the ballroom with a cello between her thighs, sadness flickering across her face as she tilted her head up, eyes still closed, her body bound to the music she created.

He should stand up, rejoin the crowd. Yes, he'd wanted different, new, exciting. But the lust simmering below the surface for a woman he'd just seen was a little too heated, like a fire about to break free and burst into a raging inferno. Yes, he wanted change.

He also wanted—needed—to stay in control.

He started to stand up, to resume visiting with politicians, billionaires and movie stars. To walk away from the temptation that had unexpectedly wrapped around him and sunk talons deep into his skin.

Then the music stopped. Noises still filled the ballroom—glasses clinking, a man laughing a little too loudly, heels clicking on the marble floor. People continued on as if nothing had changed.

The musician opened her eyes. From this distance, he couldn't discern the color. He watched as she leaned over, acknowledged something another musician said with a small smile. Damon's event planner took to the stage to announce a fifteen-minute break between the symphony and the next band that would play.

The cellist propped her instrument on a stand and stood. Slight of figure, a little shorter than he'd anticipated but strength evident in the set of her shoulders, the confident tilt of her chin.

Then she looked up. Their gazes collided, held as something electric sizzled between them.

Oh, yes. He should definitely walk away, back into the safety of the crowds and the people who wanted nothing more than a minute of his time or a few millions of his fortune.

But, he thought with a sudden wild abandon, where was the fun in that?

Evolet Grey walked back into the ballroom and, despite her best intentions, found her eyes drifting to the small alcove at the edge of the space. Awareness filled her body as her eyes connected once more with that of the handsome behemoth of a man lounging in a wingback chair. Others might've perceived his posture as relaxed, but he reminded her of a predator lying in wait, deceptively calm as he waited for his prey to come closer. A shiver danced down her spine, but God help her, she couldn't look away.

Her gaze traveled down over his black tuxedo, stark against the white of the chair, and then back up to his face. Notes danced in her head, landing on the imaginary staff lines she'd conjured and creating a brooding, sensual melody for the mystery man in the alcove.

Classically handsome. Dark brown hair worn thick

on top and short on the sides. The aloof expression on his square face, coupled with the slight hollows beneath his cheekbones, made him seem cold, distant.

Except for his eyes. A hint of something wild lurked beneath the tightly buttoned-up surface.

That hint of wild did funny things to her insides. Like quicken her heartbeat and make heat pool low in her belly.

Stop.

She looked away, cutting off the naughty direction of her errant thoughts. She made her way over to the bar closest to the stage. It wasn't every day she got to have a drink in a hotel like the Winchester. The ballroom was a little more modern than she'd prefer, with soaring pillars and floor-to-ceiling windows that overlooked Central Park just across the street. But still, she had to acknowledge, elegantly done up for tonight's gala. Whoever had planned tonight's event had money with a capital *M.* A dance floor of wood so dark it was almost black dominated the center of the room. White chairs and couches had been clustered around the edges, creating intimate spaces for one to escape to if they needed a breather or a quiet place to conduct business. The walls glowed with blue-and-violet lighting. A minor detail, but it managed to make the space feel intimate even though there were close to five hundred people milling about dressed in their most glamorous clothes.

A woman passed by in a backless red dress with several feet of silk trailing after her. A man walked by with an actual monocle trimmed in what she guessed were real diamonds.

Evolet's stomach did a nervous roll. This wasn't her

world. Far from it. She hadn't felt it onstage. There she had been in control, in her element. But out here, among the jewelry and the haute couture clothes and the scent of money thick in the air, she felt like a nobody.

¡Para!

A smile curved her lips as she heard her adoptive mother Constanza's husky voice in her head. She was every bit loving and supportive but had zero tolerance for self-pity and no patience for those who placed value on money rather than family.

If Constanza were here, she would have arched her razor-thin brow at the silk trailing on the floor, tsked at the waste of good material and then said something like, *You've earned your place here*, mija. *Now stop moping and enjoy yourself.*

With the much-needed boost to her self-confidence, Evolet continued across the floor. She would have a drink, enjoy a few minutes in the most elegant room she'd ever been in and then go home for a soak in the tub.

And, she thought as her smile spread, perhaps entertain a fantasy or two about the mysterious man who had made her pulse race. She'd learned from the few dates she'd been on since graduating that fantasies— at least when it came to romance—were usually more enjoyable than the actual experience.

She was almost to the bar when a hand gripped her elbow.

"Aren't you a sight for sore eyes?"

The stench of too much alcohol stung her nose. She started to turn just before an arm slid about her waist and pulled her closer to the offending smell.

"What's your name? Haven't seen you at one of these galas before."

She found herself face-to-face with a bleary-eyed blond man. His leering smile didn't quite stretch all the way, as if his lips were just as intoxicated as he was and couldn't hold themselves up.

"I'm with the symphony," she said in as polite a voice as she could muster. She grabbed his hand and pulled it off her waist while taking a deliberate step back.

"I've heard great things about musicians. Very talented hands." The suggestive lift of his eyebrows made her cringe. "Perhaps after the gala we could find out if they're true."

She barely stopped herself from gagging. Wealth obviously didn't equal class or charm. Her eyes dropped to his hands, one clutched around a martini glass, the other sporting a fancy silver watch and an ornate wedding ring.

She forced a smile onto her face even as disgust rolled in her belly. "I'm fortunate to play alongside some very gifted musicians," she replied coolly. "Unfortunately, we only perform as a group. I'm not available for private performances."

He blinked at her, a frown breaking through his intoxication. "I'm not asking for a musical," he sputtered. "I'm asking for—"

"Is that your wife?"

A look akin to fear crossed the man's face as his head whipped around. Evolet took the opportunity to lean forward, place a finger under the martini glass and lift up. A flick was all it took for the peachy-pink drink to spill onto the man's white shirt. The glass tumbled from his fingers and crashed onto the floor. The music playing from the speakers and the chattering of the guests muffled some of the commotion, but a number of people turned to see who had dropped the glass.

The man's face reddened as he looked from his shirt down to the offending pile of broken glass at his feet.

"Did you…" He looked up at her and then back down again. She almost felt bad for him as he blinked and struggled to make sense of what just happened. "Did I do that?"

"You did, Harry."

Evolet froze. The deep velvet-timbred tone came from behind and slid over her skin, sparking little fires as it wound around her and made her suck in a breath even as panic fluttered in her chest. Had the owner of the seductive voice seen her maneuver?

Harry's face paled at an astonishingly fast speed.

"Oh…um, I think I just had a little too much—"

"Harry!"

Evolet almost felt sorry for Harry when the remaining color in his face disappeared, replaced with stark white fear as a slender woman with jet-black hair piled high in an elegant arrangement of curls walked up to him, her eyes hard.

Almost.

"Darling, there you are." The woman slid her arm through Harry's, her manicured fingernails digging into the sleeve of his jacket like claws. "The Joneses have been asking after you." She aimed a brittle smile at Evolet and whoever stood behind her before dragging off a very unhappy-looking Harry.

Evolet steeled herself for whatever was behind her and turned.

You.

CHAPTER TWO

HER MYSTERY MAN stood before her, tall and dark and brooding. She tilted her chin up and met his gaze head-on. And what a gaze it was. Emerald shot through with flecks of gold, framed by thick brows that were currently drawn together as he studied her. The amused twist of his full lips told her he had seen her little maneuver.

"Thank you," she said.

One of those brows shot up.

"For what? Seems like you had everything in hand."

Heat rose in her cheeks. "It was just—"

"A clever way of dealing with an insufferable ass who drinks too much and hits on anyone who is not his wife."

Evolet bit down on her bottom lip to stop her grin.

"Well...thank you." She cast a quick glance around. Thankfully people had returned to their private conversations, and a fast-acting server had already swept up the glass. No permanent damage seemed to have been done. "I appreciate your discretion."

His lips tilted up another notch. "You're welcome." He nodded toward the bar. "Anthony is a magician when it comes to drinks. After your run-in with Harry, you could probably use one."

She focused on the menu, written in an elegant script, and not on the distracting man standing a breath away from her. "The Lavender Spy, please."

She felt the man start next to her. But when she glanced up, his face was impassive as he looked out over the crowds with a bored expression. Anthony handed her a glass filled with a pale purple drink topped off with a sprig of lavender. She thanked him and raised the glass to her lips.

"Oh, wow," she breathed as the mixture of gin, lavender and lime hit her tongue. "That's delicious."

"Do you enjoy gin often?"

"This is my first time," she replied as she took another sip. "I don't do much drinking. None at all, actually. I'm usually practicing or performing." Or working as a floating executive assistant, but she kept that part out. It was just a stop on the way to her ultimate goal of playing professionally for an orchestra. "Leaves little time for happy hour."

"How did you decide on the cello?"

The rumble of his voice rolled through her once more, deep and delicious. Her fingers tightened on her glass as butterflies fluttered in her stomach.

Down, girl.

"The first time I heard one was in the subway. I was walking and heard music. It was incredible."

The memory of it washed over her. She'd only been with Constanza a few weeks and had been pushing her then foster mother away with biting insults or cold silences. That Constanza had replied with a table heaped with traditional Haitian foods, freshly laundered clothes and a gentle smile had made her feel guilty, which had made her angrier. The walls she'd built over the years had trembled with every kind gesture, and damn it, she hadn't wanted that. She hadn't wanted to get attached when she could've been yanked away at any moment.

Which had made the deep tug in her chest as she'd heard the first haunting strains of the cello in the tunnels more powerful, as if someone was calling to her who finally understood all of her pain, her heartache and loss.

She'd followed the music through the people crowding the tunnels at rush hour. Everything else had faded: the rumble of the trains, the cacophony of voices, the incessant beeping and ringing of phones.

There had only been the music.

"Like angels singing?"

She blinked and refocused on the man with a frown.

"No, the opposite. He was…" Her hand came up, her fingers moving in the air as she mimicked the movements she'd seen the day her world had changed. The day she'd stopped surviving and started living. "He was making the cello weep."

"Weep?"

She took another drink to cover her wince. Not the most PR-friendly way of describing the beginning of her music career. These people wanted glitz and glamour, not sad and depressing.

But something in the way he looked at her, with an intensity that made her feel as if he could see beneath all the years of practice, made her want to tell him. To share what had led her from a tiny two-bedroom apartment in East Harlem to performing in a string orchestra in one of the ritziest hotels in New York City.

Don't do it.

Hadn't she learned her lesson over the years? Trusting and confiding in someone opened the door to getting one's hopes up. To getting hurt. Constanza had been a miracle, a gift she'd never expected to receive, but also a rarity. No one before or since had been there for her.

The reminder helped her rein in her memories. She let out a light laugh.

"Musicians can be a bit dramatic. I enjoyed the music. The cellist was kind enough to answer my questions after he played. I started taking lessons, and here I am," she finished with a gesture to one of the nearby glass cocktail tables topped off with white blooms and flickering candles.

The man's frown deepened. "That's not what you were going to say."

Now it was her turn to frown, partially at his firm tone and partially at his bold words. Had she misread him?

"Excuse me?"

He leaned in, but unlike with Harry, his closeness didn't inspire disgust. It made her breath catch in her chest and that damned heat burn hotter, intoxicating even as she silently cursed it. She did not want to be attracted to anyone, let alone a rich playboy who probably dated models and actresses and politicians.

Someone who would never look twice at someone like her.

The urge to flee descended on her rapidly. Her pulse started to flutter, and she cast about for a reason to leave as the lead singer of the band called everyone to join him on the dance floor. Her lips parted, some inane excuse drifting up. She nearly dropped her own drink when his fingers closed firmly about her hand. Her head jerked up, and she read in his eyes that he knew she'd been about to walk away.

"Dance with me."

Evolet had always thought nothing could be more seductive than the sounds of her cello. More than one man had accused her of being a cold fish, a criticism she'd taken in stride because no man had ever enticed her beyond a second date or an unsatisfying kiss good-night. Ever since she'd wandered down a subway tunnel at fifteen in search of a song that had called to her, only two things had mattered to her in the world: Constanza and her cello.

But now, as his invitation penetrated her shock, she had the unsettling feeling of her world shifting. If she said yes, it would shift even further. She wouldn't see this man beyond this night. Yet she would always carry the memory of his touch, the remembrance of his hand wrapped possessively around hers.

And the lingering memory of what a dance with him would have been like.

"All right."

Before she questioned her own judgment, before she could even blink, he plucked her drink from her hand, set it back down on the bar and, with a light touch of fingers on the small of her back that burned through the material of her dress, whisked her onto the dance floor.

"You've done that before."

He gave her a wolfish smile. "Done what?"

His fingers firmed against her back, the palm of his

hand pressing her body closer to his. His other hand captured one of hers in a gentle grasp, as if he knew if he squeezed too tightly she would leave. The contact of skin against skin made her dizzier than any embrace or kiss she'd ever experienced.

"Seduced a woman to dance with you," she said breathlessly.

Fire flashed in his eyes. "Do you feel like I'm seducing you…?" His voice trailed off as he arched a brow. "I don't know your name."

"Likewise," she retorted. She was rewarded with a deep rumble of laughter that seemed to surprise both of them.

"Let's trade, shall we?"

Her eyes drifted down to his mouth. His smile stole some of the shadows from his eyes. What would it be like to kiss him? To taste his lips against hers, open her mouth to his and—

"Trade?" she whispered.

His smile widened, and her chest tightened.

"You tell me your name. I'll tell you mine."

Oh, no, she was *enjoying* this. Enjoying the banter with a handsome, wealthy man who, for whatever reason, was interested in talking to her. For someone who wasn't used to being wanted in any capacity, to have a man want to dance with her, to spend time with her, was exhilarating.

The tempo of the music picked up. Uncertainty made her stumble. The man's hand tightened on hers, steadying her.

"Relax."

"It's hard when I don't know what I'm doing."

"Trust me."

He said it with humor in his voice. But his gaze was intense, piercing through the armor she kept wrapped around herself. Torn between vulnerability and defiance, she paused.

Until one corner of his mouth quirked up in that sexy half smile. Daring her.

She raised her chin as she forced herself to ease into his embrace. As he spun her into a turn, she leaned into him. The first moment was terrifying. When was the last time she had surrendered control, trusted someone else?

But he didn't give her time to be afraid. He took advantage of her submission and spun her into another turn with a bold confidence that brought an entranced smile to her lips. He replied with a smile of his own that transformed his brooding attractiveness into one of devastating handsomeness.

He led her through the rest of the dance with strength and skill. Most of the other dancers swayed back and forth. A few attempted similar moves as her mystery man, but none replicated his talent.

As the music wound down, Evolet arched a brow. "Are you a professional ballroom dancer?"

He chuckled. "Far from it. That is the one dance I know how to do well."

"Very well."

"My mother was a good teacher."

The humor in his eyes dimmed, replaced by an emotion Evolet knew all too well.

Anguish.

"What happened to her?" she asked softly.

His gaze slid back to her. In the span of a breath, Evolet saw it all: heartbreak, agony, despair.

Then his stare hardened, freezing out the emotions displayed so nakedly just a moment ago. This time his smile was practiced, one she'd spied on the faces of the other richly attired men in the ballroom.

"I'll get you a fresh drink."

She felt the rejection like a slap. She stepped back, frowning when he took his time releasing her from his hold. Their interlude had been wonderful, a fairy tale come true for a drink and a dance.

And now it was over. She'd learned her lesson and stopped reaching for the stars when it came to relationships and people. Some stars would always be too far out of reach. That she had wanted their time together to last longer than the song they'd danced to made it even more imperative that she leave now. When it came to people, wanting and hoping were fatal flaws. People died, like her father. People left, like her mother. Constanza had left her in the end, even if it hadn't been her choice.

People were unpredictable. Uncontrollable. They could inflict pain, even if they didn't mean to.

Evolet's eyes drifted back to the stage. The memory of the gleaming wood of her cello calmed the tumultuous emotions tangling and fighting for dominance in her chest. She could depend on her cello, her talents and her own hard work.

Yes, she'd been able to depend on her dark-haired stranger for a dance. She hadn't even realized that she had entertained a brief fantasy that their time together would extend beyond the music. But he had reminded her with his swift rejection of her inquiry that there was nothing between them but the novelty of a few minutes spent together in a luxurious surrounding. He'd find her interesting tonight, perhaps a little longer. Then his curiosity would pass, along with the uniqueness of the company of a struggling cellist. He would return to his world, and she'd return to hers.

She had no desire to experience that emotional roller coaster. Especially, she acknowledged reluctantly, because this man had the potential to leave her with some deep scars on her already battered heart.

"It's late," she said in answer to his frown.

He glanced down at his watch. The stainless steel band glinted under the lights of the chandelier. Probably cost more than her cello.

"It's just past eight o'clock."

"And it'll take me an hour to get home." She held out her hand. "Thank you for the dance."

She knew she'd made a mistake the moment his fingers enveloped hers in a firm grip. The sensation of his skin sliding against hers made her gasp. Her heart pounded so fiercely she wondered if he could hear it above the music.

Yet when her eyes darted up to his face, it was to meet an impenetrable emerald gaze that doused the lingering sparks of her attraction.

"Enjoy the rest of your evening," he said coolly.

She nodded and turned away, then wove her way among the dancers as she tried to keep her pace steady so it didn't look like she was running. She breathed in deeply and summoned her mental checklist. The music, clinks of glasses and murmurs of conversation faded as she ran down her tasks: collect her cello, grab her coat, walk to the Fifty-Ninth Street subway station.

She'd almost made it to the edge of the ballroom when temptation reared its evil little head. With a resigned sigh, she looked over her shoulder for one last glance at the opulence she'd enjoyed and, perhaps, the man who had briefly whisked her into a fantasy.

Another mistake, she realized belatedly. He stood on the opposite side of the ballroom, a fresh drink in hand, leaning against the bar with a casual, aloof stance as two women in stunning evening gowns talked to him. The redhead laid her hand on the sleeve of his jacket in a gesture Evolet recognized as the move of a woman who had found something she wanted.

Her stomach sank. Ridiculous to experience jealousy over a man she had just met—and would never meet again. Even more foolish to be disappointed that her suspicion that she was nothing more than a blip in his wealthy existence had been proven accurate.

He looked up, and she bit back a gasp as he stared right at her. Desire flared low in her belly before burning a trail through her veins. Images filled her mind, of bodies tangled together in a carnal dance far more intimate than the one they had just shared.

The erotic vividness of her fantasy shocked her. Her lips parted, and despite the distance between them, she saw his gaze darken. Was it her imagination, or did the air around her grow heavy, pressing on her skin with the promise of what could be between them?

Between you and a man you barely know?

She grabbed on to the thin thread of sanity that broke through. A man who, in less than ten minutes, she'd shared one of the most defining moments of her life with.

No matter what existed between them for a night, a

man like that would walk away with a woman's heart and never look back.

Evolet turned and fled.

CHAPTER THREE

DAMON HIT END on the call and let out a slow, satisfied breath. His lips quirked up at the corners as his blood hummed with pride. Bradford Global was in the final three for the manufacturing of Royal Air's upcoming fleet of jets.

Based out of Sweden, Royal Air had taken the travel world by storm ten years ago. They'd released a line of luxury planes that offered amenities on their transatlantic flights no longer found elsewhere unless someone had the good fortune, literally, to afford a first-class ticket. Three-course meals served on china plates, a complimentary cocktail and enough space for passengers over five feet tall—all at the same rates as their competitors—had catapulted them to superstardom.

Now they were building ten new planes, to be completed in two years or less as Royal Air's contract stipulated. With each plane worth close to $130 million dollars, it was a contract that had ignited fierce competition.

Winning the contract would be the ultimate achievement of his tenure as head of Bradford Global.

He glanced back at the hotel, at the glittering people wandering in and out of the bank of glass doors that lined the main entrance facing West Fifty-Ninth Street and the southern end of Central Park. There were some people inside he genuinely liked, some he even considered friends.

None of them would understand the value of the Royal Air contract beyond the dollar signs attached to it. In moments like this, the faint pain that lingered just out of sight swelled into an ache that wrapped around his heart and squeezed so hard he had to force himself to breathe deeply.

Fourteen years. Fourteen years he had led Bradford Global. Fourteen years' worth of holidays and other important milestones he'd spent alone. Most of the time, he could keep the pain at bay. But tonight, more than anything, he wanted his parents by his side, to share the news and revel in how far Bradford Global had come, from a small plant in Illinois to being considered for Royal Air's luxury airplane contract, one of the most coveted projects in the manufacturing world.

Brown eyes ringed in gold appeared in his mind, with humor glimmering in their tawny depths. Damon's fingers tightened around his phone. He'd let down his guard tonight with the mysterious cellist. She'd intrigued him the moment those first haunting notes of her solo had carried across the ballroom and grabbed hold of something deep inside him. His interest had been furthered by her amusing way of handling Harry Dumont's drunken attempts at seduction.

Although his own flirtation had surprised him. He had no interest in long-term relationships, in marriage. Losing his parents had severed most of his interest in loving another person. He'd found salvation from his pain, his nightmares of the hell of his parents' final moments, in work, in things he could control.

If there had been any lingering desire for something like what his parents had enjoyed, it had been torpedoed by the kind of women he'd dated or associated with professionally. His last lover, Natalie Robinson, was the daughter of a senator. Refined, driven in her work as a marketer for a prominent hospital. Yet her true colors had shown as soon as he'd shown an ounce of leeway and allowed her to keep some things at his Park Avenue penthouse. On Valentine's Day less than two months later, she'd pounced like a predator and told him she had decided they were getting married.

Damon still thought about her sometimes when he walked past Cartier on Fifth Avenue and the $1.2 million ring they had tried to charge him for the next day. He'd sent her the bill and a professional mover with her things neatly packed in cardboard boxes. She'd accused him in a series of text messages and one nasty voice mail of being cold, of never opening up and forcing her to take action. He hadn't corrected her. He was cold. He had no interest in opening up, of being emotionally vulnerable to anyone.

Emotions couldn't be controlled. Emotions were chaos.

But he was more than capable of conducting a discreet, enjoyable affair without letting himself succumb to feelings.

He glanced back at the hotel once more. He'd been rude when she'd asked about his mother. He hadn't intended to be. His initial reaction had been one of surprised pleasure that someone would ask about her. That was by his choice, he reminded himself. He had made it clear to everyone, from his uncle and distant family to employees and lovers, that his parents were not to be a topic of conversation.

The realization that he'd done both himself and his parents a disservice by burying their memory had unnerved him. As had the sudden desire to tell a woman he'd just met what had happened the night a college student had drunk one too many, gotten behind the wheel and taken his family from him.

It was that want to share with her that had made him step back. He'd seen the hurt in her eyes, felt an uncomfortable prick of guilt that she had shared a moment that was obviously personal to her while he'd kept his walls firmly in place.

Irritated, he shoved his phone into his pocket and looked back out over the sea of taxis, limos and other vehicles inching their way along the road. He had no reason to feel guilty. She was, after all, just a woman he'd shared a drink and a dance with. She'd made the choice to share her past. He'd made the choice not to.

His logic failed to dislodge the discomfort that lingered on the edges of his satisfaction with Bradford Global's latest accomplishment.

With a softly muttered oath, he turned around to go back inside and do his due diligence as CEO. Make the rounds, shake some hands, keep Tracy Montebach's manicured talons off him and…

His checklist faded as the cellist walked out of the hotel. Incredible what the simple act of letting one's hair down could do. He'd already been intrigued by the mix of elfish softness and sharp angles in her face, displayed prominently when her hair was pulled back into the tight bun.

Now her hair fell in golden waves just past her shoulders as she stopped at the edge of the sidewalk. The casual disarray of soft curls sent a bolt of heat straight to his groin.

She looked up and down the street, probably searching for a cab, one hand wrapped around the strap of her purse, the other carrying her cello case. He was close enough to the building that he'd escaped her notice so far. He took advantage and let his eyes rake over the confident set of her shoulders, the flattering cling of a black trench coat belted at her narrow waist, her elegant legs clad in black tights, which were a far more sensual sight than Tracy's plunging neckline.

What would she look like, he mused as her head turned toward Central Park, *in red? Or gold, to match her eyes?*

Black suited her, added a layer of mystique. But it also made her seem aloof, distant, like an exquisite painting or sculpture one might gaze on in a museum.

Untouchable.

Which was for the best, he reminded himself as she crossed the street and started down the sidewalk. She intrigued him too much to be worth the risk of getting to know her better.

His resolution dissolved like a puff of smoke as she turned onto Center Drive, walked past the collection of horse-drawn carriages lingering on the street and disappeared into Central Park.

He stared for a moment. She'd struck him as an intelligent woman. Surely she wouldn't be so foolish as to walk in Central Park alone at night.

But she didn't reappear.

Before he could question himself, his feet carried

him across the street, down the sidewalk and into the park. Her meandering pace and the giant cello case in hand made it easy to reach her side.

"Where are you going?"

She glanced over her shoulder, surprise passing over her face before her features settled into a wary frown.

"Walking through the park. What are you doing out here? Did you follow me?"

"I was outside taking a call when I saw you leave. You're walking in Central Park at night?"

"Yes."

"Why not catch a cab?"

Her frown deepened. "Cabs are expensive."

"Then I'll get you one."

The frown morphed into an expression of thunderous indignation. If he hadn't been so irritated at her lack of critical thinking, he would have taken a moment to enjoy the vivid play of emotions across her face.

"Don't you dare. I'm not paying you back for a cab when I have two perfectly good feet for walking."

"It's dangerous."

She sighed as if he had annoyed her. He fought to keep his own annoyance under control. She had no idea who he was, that he could easily buy her a hundred cellos or a damned limo to ferry her around the city. How many people back at the gala would snort with laughter if they knew a musician had offered to pay back the CEO of Bradford Global for a cab ride?

"I wouldn't have pegged you for one of those," she said, her disappointed tone rubbing against his skin like sandpaper.

"One what?"

"A worrywart."

"I am not a worrywart," he replied, trying—and failing—to keep his own indignation out of his voice.

"Yes, you are." She gestured to the lantern-lined road that ran through the southern end of the park. "I'm talking about walking down Center Drive surrounded by people, not dashing through the trees on some unlit path."

A valid point, he inwardly conceded as people strode by. Couples walking hand in hand, a few families, cyclists and some tourists with cameras. A police car drove slowly down the lane.

But as she stood there, backlit by the lanterns and holding her ridiculously oversized cello case in her small hands, he didn't want to let her out of his sight.

"Are you walking all the way home?"

"No." She said the word slowly, as if she couldn't believe his stupidity. "That would take me hours. I'm walking to Sixty-Eighth Street station. I decided I wanted to walk through Central Park because it's nice outside, the park looked beautiful and, oh, yeah, because I wanted to." One hand stayed clenched around the handle of her case, the other landing on her hip as her eyes narrowed. "Why a man I just met and shared one dance with needs to know all that, I have no idea. But now that you do, are you satisfied?"

Her last word rippled across his skin, rekindled the arousal she had stirred in the ballroom, then again on the sidewalk. How holding her in his arms, feeling her body lean into his with complete trust, had made him want to peel away that bulky black dress and trace his fingers over her naked skin. He had always left his previous lovers satisfied.

But with this woman, it wasn't just courtesy mixed

with male pride that had him wanting to see her lips parted on a moan of pleasure, her eyes glazed as he stroked and kissed and savored. No, it was something more primal. Not just a want, but a need.

No, he thought, *I am nowhere near satisfied.*

"I don't like you walking through the park alone at night."

"You don't have to. Good night."

And then she turned and walked away.

Damon stared after her, barely keeping his mouth from dropping open in surprise. No one walked away from him. Ever.

Part of him wanted to let her go. She didn't want his help—fine. She was obviously used to doing things on her own without help from anyone.

The perfect opportunity to let her walk away, out of his life, and take temptation with her.

Except he couldn't. He told himself it was because he couldn't allow a woman to walk in Central Park alone, no matter how many strides the city had taken toward security and public safety. Told himself escorting her to the station was the polite thing to do.

He steadfastly ignored the rush of heat through his veins that told him there was something much more dangerous pushing him on and followed his cellist into Central Park.

Evolet cursed under her breath as her heartbeat sped up at the sound of his footsteps on the path behind her. She didn't know which she had hoped for more—that he would follow her or that he wouldn't. Judging by the slight hitch in her breath as he fell into step beside her and that sensual, rich scent of sage and wood, her body had hoped for the former.

Embarrassment at his questioning had made her irritation with her self-appointed protector more poignant, her tone sharper than she had intended. And even though she certainly didn't need looking after, he was just trying to help. The women he associated with were probably waited on hand and foot by servants, chauffeurs and the like. He wouldn't be used to a woman who had moved from house to house every year or so, her meager belongings shoved into a threadbare pillowcase as she said goodbye over and over again until she hadn't been able to say goodbye anymore. Instead, she'd withdrawn into herself, become sullen and angry, ignoring the overtures of her well-meaning foster parents until they gave up and counted down the days until she was moved again.

No, her mysterious escort wouldn't have experience with women like her at all.

Walking five minutes to the station nearest the hotel would have been the practical thing to do. But tonight, she didn't want to be practical. She'd been practical for so long, shelving her fantasies for more pragmatic endeavors. Even her dream of becoming a professional cellist had evolved into something sensible, a goal to be achieved instead of a wish to be fulfilled. A subtle difference, but one that had left her a hollow shell of herself.

The artist in her had been stifled, the dreamer left adrift in a sea of rationality.

Just for tonight, she wanted to indulge the romantic side she hid behind walls constructed of black clothing and old wounds. The same desire that had made her say yes to a dance with a stranger had guided her feet into the park as her heart cried out for the magic of a walk among the budding trees and lantern-lit walkways.

But the brooding man at her side wouldn't see the magic. No, he struck her as the kind of man who would be more comfortable with facts, numbers and reports.

What did he do for a living, she mused, as he stalked alongside her. Dressed in a tailored suit and a guest at one of the most prominent fundraisers of the year, he was most likely a somebody with a capital *S*. He was an intriguing mix of contradictions: proper in his expensive tux, yet rakish with those top buttons undone. Arrogant in his overall demeanor, but kind enough to walk a virtual stranger through Central Park at night instead of enjoying cocktails and hors d'oeuvres at a fancy gala.

Don't get too involved, Grey.

Except he made it very hard to keep her mind from wandering to what-ifs when he insisted on doing nice, if misguided, things like walking her to the subway.

His dark, brooding handsomeness, coupled with that slow-burning smile he'd tossed her way a couple times, didn't help, either.

"Can I at least know the name of my knight in shining armor?"

Several seconds passed before he finally said, "Damon."

The name conjured up a smoky ballad, one simmering with repressed power and raw strength.

"Reminds me of the little boy from that horror movie."

Damon's chuckle rippled across her skin. "Are you calling me the son of the devil?"

"I don't know you well enough to know that."

Although with the way he tempted her, she could easily picture him in such a role.

"And you?" When she looked up at him, he arched one brow. "Who am I escorting?"

"Evie."

She went with the name Constanza had called her for years. Something kept her from divulging her full name, from sharing even more of herself with this man who tied her up in knots.

"Where do you live, Evie?"

She rolled her eyes at his persistence. "I never answer that question on a first date."

She winced. *Not a date.*

"Do you go on many first dates?"

"Not really."

"Why not?"

"I'm usually practicing, auditioning or performing." She lifted her cello case up. "Constance is my only love." She looked over to see Damon's lips quirk up.

"Constance?"

Words rested on the tip of her tongue, words to honor the woman who had become her mother. How Constanza had grown and sold geraniums on the fire escape to help pay for Evolet's first cello. The husky, delighted laugh when Evolet had played her first piece. The hands crinkled like paper as they'd wiped away Evolet's tears after her first failed audition.

But she stopped herself. It wasn't just that she'd already shared so much with a man who had made it clear he was sharing nothing. Thinking of Constanza trapped in the nursing home, succumbing to the illness of her own mind as disease slowly leeched away what little she had left, made Evolet want to scream and rage at the world. It had given her the one thing she had wanted more than anything—a family—and was now cruelly snatching it away.

"My adoptive mother. Her name is Constanza."

"It looks heavy."

"It is, but I'm the only one who carries it." She hurried on before he could press her for details. "What about you? Any lonely hearts waiting for you back at the gala? Perhaps two," she added impishly, even though she didn't like the image of the redheaded woman's hand on Damon's arm nor the jealousy that curled low in her stomach.

"Tracy Montebach and a friend whose name escapes me. Probably latched on to her newest prey."

The knot in her chest loosened at his casual dismissal. "So it's not true love?"

His deep laugh rippled over her skin once more and slid into her senses. The rich sound transformed his expression of cool elegance to devastatingly handsome as his teeth flashed white in the darkness and his eyes crinkled at the corners.

"I don't think Tracy would know love if it bit her. And," he added, "love isn't a part of my future."

"Ever?"

"Ever."

The finality in his voice made her look up. His face had smoothed into a blank mask, his eyes cold once more.

"There's a story there," she observed.

"Yes."

She wanted to push, to ask who or what had turned him away from love. But she had no desire to relive the rejection she'd experienced in the ballroom. She let his final word hang in the air between them as they continued on through the park.

As they crossed a bridge above one of the numerous paths that crisscrossed through the park, Evolet's feet slowed. She stopped and leaned over the railing, looking down at the carousel below. Golden lights glowed within the redbrick structure that housed the ride. Calliope music sang through the trees as horses soared up and down. At this hour there were only a handful of people on the carousel: two men with a little girl and a couple who seemed more interested in each other than the horses.

Damon joined her at the railing, silent and contemplative. His presence unsettled her, as did the comfort she found in standing beside him. So often she was alone. Over time, she had come to prefer it.

But right now, gazing down at one of her favorite places in the city with a complete stranger who had slid past her usual defenses, she understood at least some of the allure of sharing one's secrets with another.

"I haven't been here in years."

"Did you ever ride it?" she asked.

"Yes. Once, when I was little. For my fifth birthday, I think."

"No big party?"

"No." He paused. "My parents were down-to-earth despite their wealth. They never forgot where they came from."

She sensed that the words cost him somehow, as if he never spoke of his parents. She also heard the unspoken apology for his earlier dismissal in the ballroom and accepted it. How could she judge him for wanting to keep what was obviously a great source of pain close when she did the same every day?

He nodded toward the carousel as it slowed. "Did your parents ever bring you here?"

"No," she managed to whisper past the thickness in her throat. She watched as the fathers helped their daughter dismount from a chestnut horse with a violet saddle, her gleeful laughter rising up as the music wound down. The man with his girlfriend placed his hands on her waist and helped her down, then kissed her forehead as her feet hit the floor.

Oddly, the day she'd first laid eyes on the carousel had been the day the social worker had bought her ice cream on their way to her first foster home. A consolation prize to help her deal with her mother's abandonment. The ice cream cart had been parked just off the drive that meandered through the southern end of the park. She'd wandered over to the railing on the bridge, almost to this very spot, and looked down to see kids giggling as the carousel had spun round and round. Parents had laughed, snapped photos and hugged their children.

Love. Security. Family. Things she had craved for years.

She turned away and continued down the sidewalk, suddenly feeling foolish and shy that she'd almost shared her story with him. Damon caught up to her, his inquisitive gaze hot on her face. He knew there was more lurking beneath the surface, something deeper than just pausing to watch a carousel spin around.

"Thanks for indulging me," she said lightly.

He nodded, and she released a relieved breath that he didn't press.

They walked along in silence for a moment, crossing the road and continuing on another path that wound through trees full of unfurling green leaves and down steps framed by tall grasses.

"There's a story there."

She nearly stumbled on the last step as he repeated her words. He caught her with one hand, his fingers strong and firm on her elbow.

"What?" she whispered.

"The carousel." He cocked his head, his handsome features dusted with gold light from the lanterns. "It means something to you."

"Or maybe it just looked pretty."

Before he could respond to her retort, a single raindrop fell. She held out her hand and smiled up at the dark sky, grateful for the reprieve.

"It wasn't supposed to rain tonight," he grumbled with a glower aimed skyward.

"It's just water."

He cast a glance at the case clutched in her hand. "Aren't you worried about your cello?"

"If this were a downpour, yes. But it's just a light spring rain. I don't spend money on a lot of things, but I spent a small fortune to make sure this case was waterproof."

Lightning flickered above, followed by a soft growl of thunder. Evolet looked up to the sky. She had behaved herself for so long, forcing her dreams and longings deep down where they were safe, untouchable by the capricious and too often cruel nature of the world.

But not tonight. Tonight was about fairy tales and fantasies, dances with handsome strangers and elegant ballrooms.

The rain started to fall in earnest, a gentle whisper that kissed her skin. For the third time that night, she followed impulse and tilted her head back to the sky to embrace the storm.

Rain fell onto Evie's face, a dozen glistening drops that glimmered like diamonds. Her lips curved into a carefree, happy smile as a laugh bubbled up like champagne.

She was beautiful. Captivating. In this moment, he knew he was seeing the real Evie. And by God, she was dazzling.

When he slid an arm around her waist, her laughter faded. Her eyes met his. A lifetime passed in the span of a heartbeat as he waited for an answer to his unspoken question, gave her the opportunity to pull away. Her answer, her body softly pressing against his, ignited a firestorm in his veins that couldn't be stopped. He lowered his lips and claimed hers.

The first brush of lips was teasing, testing. She moaned softly, and his control quivered. He swept a wet curl off her cheek before his fingers tangled in her hair. Her mouth firmed beneath his, her body pressing closer. If the feeling of wet cloth could inspire such a deep need to touch, to taste, what would feeling her naked skin against his do?

His tongue teased the seam of her mouth. When her lips parted on a sigh, he tasted her, taking them both deeper. The kiss changed, grew more intense as her hands slid up his neck. Who knew the stroke of a woman's fingertips, the tug as her fingers tightened in his hair, could drive him to the edge?

The spring air grew colder as the rain fell. But here,

in the middle of a park in a city of millions, passion blazed hotter than anything he'd ever experienced. The coolness of the rain only made him more aware of the heat between him and this woman he'd just met. This woman who seemed to look past his defenses and straight into his heart.

A dangerous woman.

Her hips rocked against his in a rhythm he dimly recognized as instinct over finesse. The knowledge that she wanted him so much urged him on. He growled against her mouth, savored her cry as his hands moved down to cup her rear and haul her closer. She gasped as his hard length pressed against her most intimate flesh.

Dimly, he realized she was trembling. It nearly killed him to loosen his grip.

"Don't stop, Damon."

Her whispered plea stripped him bare. He crushed her lips beneath his again as he bound her against him in an iron hold. His hands and mouth touched her with a possessiveness he'd never experienced with anyone. They spiraled upward, wrapped in the feel of each other's bodies, the taste of each other's desire. A dream he never wanted to wake from.

A dream interrupted by shrill laughter from the rain-slicked path behind them.

"Come on, it's this cute little—oh."

Damon raised his head and saw two teenage girls standing behind them. The dim light from a nearby lantern did little to hide the embarrassed look of fascination on the face of one or the delighted smirk on the other.

"Sorry," the smug one said, not looking sorry at all. "Have fun."

Another burst of laughter and they were gone.

Slowly, Damon turned to look down into gold eyes wide with shock. Her lips were swollen, her breathing ragged as she clung to his arms like she might collapse without his support.

"Evie, I…"

The whisper of her name on his lips seemed to shock her back to life. She wrenched herself from him, gathered up her cello case and lurched down the steps carved into the hillside.

"Wait!"

His command whipped out, one that some of the wealthiest men in the world would have heeded. But it had no effect on her as she dashed away into the night. Damon stared at the empty path as the storm pounded harder, flattening the tall stalks of grasses and wildflowers edging the walkway. The part of him she had bewitched with her gold eyes and bold, if not foolish, bravado as she'd traipsed through Central Park demanded he follow. His rational side, the part that had ruled for over a decade, ordered him to let her go. She was an adult. She'd made her choice to leave.

By the time he gave in to desire and stalked down the steps and back onto a paved path, she was gone.

Swallowed up by the darkness and the rain.

CHAPTER FOUR

EVOLET'S FINGERS TIGHTENED around her coffee as the subway car swayed. The train curved around a corner, wheels screeching in protest. Commuters leaned with the turn, eyes fixed on phones or books or companions. An out-of-town family chattered away about the lengthy list of tourist spots on their itinerary.

Another Monday on the subway, Evolet thought with a small smile as she inhaled the dark, delicious scent wafting up from her cup. Her second coffee of the morning.

Normally she pinched pennies and made her own coffee. But the rich aroma of roasted beans and coffee grounds had lured her to the open-air market beneath the Park Avenue train tracks. That and the exhaustion no amount of sleep seemed to defeat.

It didn't help that every time she had closed her eyes she'd been plagued with memories of Damon's lips moving over hers, arms like steel pressing her closer to his warmth.

Or, worst of all, the echo of his groan slipping into her veins, drugging her with the knowledge that he had wanted her. She'd woken more than once hot and tangled in her sheets.

The subway gave another lurch. Coffee splashed onto her hand. With a muffled curse, she reached into her pocket for one of the napkins the perky barista had insisted she take. She looked up to see a young girl watching her with wide eyes. Feeling guilty over her verbal slipup, she gave the girl a wink and was rewarded with a gap-toothed smile.

The subway, Evolet had long ago decided, got a bad rap. Not only had the tunnels winding beneath the legion of skyscrapers led her to her passion, but they were fun.

Judging by the disapproving scowl on Damon's face when she had mentioned the subway, he had not experienced its underrated pleasures.

The man, and his incredible mouth, wouldn't stay out of her thoughts.

But, she acknowledged with a smile as an electronic voice announced her station, it had had unexpected benefits. She'd visited Constanza at the nursing home Saturday morning, then spent Saturday afternoon and most of Sunday in the park practicing. For the first time, she hadn't poured pain and mourning and loss into her music. It had been passion that had ruled her bow, desire that had coaxed sultry notes from her cello. Playing had been an almost erotic experience, one that had left her warm and flushed by the time she was done.

It had been her best practice session in years. She hoped dearly that the next time she got an audition, they would allow independent showcases in addition to the music often chosen by the orchestras.

Until then, however, she also needed to make some rent money. Which was why, she thought with a resigned sigh as she moved with the crush of bodies toward the doorway and stepped onto the concrete platform, she had accepted the last-minute request for an executive assistant from the temp agency she worked for. Her talents for organizing, concise communication and getting things done quickly had come in handy when she'd started working for NYC Executives Inc., a temporary employment agency that specialized in executive assistants, secretaries and receptionists. She'd worked for airlines, shipping companies, hotels, restaurants, even a theater. Certainly not her passion, but the temporary nature of her work kept things interesting. Most importantly, it paid well.

The call had come in at six a.m. that morning from Miranda, one of the heads at the agency. The executive assistant for a high-ranking executive at Bradford Global had gone into labor overnight and welcomed her bundle of joy four weeks early. With a potentially lucrative contract from a European airline company on the line, the officer, a Ms. Laura Roberts, needed all the help she could get preparing for the final round of bidding.

When Miranda had said the name of the company, Damon's handsome face had flashed through Evolet's mind, along with a jolt of panic. He hadn't said he worked for the company, and there had been plenty of people there affiliated with other organizations. But what if he did? What if she ran into him in the halls or had to work with him?

Typing *Damon* into Bradford Global's website had netted a zero. She hadn't known whether to be relieved or disappointed.

Focus. She would be working with Ms. Roberts for

at least two months. Entertaining thoughts of an incredibly sexy, brooding guest from Bradford Global's gala was the opposite of professional. Being an executive assistant wasn't her dream job, but it was a job and one she did well.

With her resolution of banishing thoughts of Damon from her mind, she marched up the stairs into the weak light of early morning sunshine. The Financial District of Lower Manhattan vibrated with activity. Buildings of various heights lined the road, from limestone behemoths nearly a hundred years old to brand-new creations of steel and glass.

Bradford Global occupied the top floor of the Pomme Building, a newly constructed high-rise that dominated the city's skyline. An elevator whisked her up to the seventieth floor. The doors whooshed open to a lobby with dark wood floors, wrought iron chandeliers that looked as if they'd been fashioned out of black piping and brown leather chairs that encouraged one to sink into their buttery-soft depths with a good book. The floor-to-ceiling windows overlooking Midtown offset the darkness of the decor and offered a view that nearly made her jaw drop.

Not, Evolet mused, what she had expected. Based on the lavish wealth on display at Friday night's event, she'd anticipated lots of sterile white and modern, hard-edged furnishings. Not the cozy and welcoming atmosphere of a library.

A massive desk stood off to one side with the company's logo emblazoned on the front. The woman sitting behind the desk was more Evolet's idea of what the guard to a multibillion-dollar company looked like. Late fifties to early sixties, but, oh, Evolet hoped she looked that good as she aged. With a sleekly cut blond bob that framed elegant cheekbones, diamond studs glinting at her ears and a slender form clad in a navy sheath dress, the woman was the definition of class.

Before Evolet could tug nervously at ties on her blouse, the woman stood and shot Evolet a bright smile that lit up her face, the crinkling around her eyes softening her expression.

"Welcome to Bradford Global. I'm Julie, the front secretary. You must be Evolet Grey." At Evolet's raised eyebrows, Julie chuckled. "Security notified me you were on your way up."

Julie's bubbly voice and the soft twang of an accent Evolet couldn't quite place loosened the tension that usually accompanied her on the first day of a new assignment.

"Thank you," she said with an answering smile. "I'm excited to be with you all for the next couple of months. Although I hope the woman I'm replacing and her baby are all right?"

Julie beamed with approval as she pulled her phone out of her pocket.

"Aren't you sweet to ask. They're doing wonderfully." She showed Evolet a picture of an exhausted but very happy looking woman in a hospital gown with a tiny baby cradled in her arms. "Gave us a bit of a fright with how early she came, but Louise did beautifully." Her grin broadened. "Your contract might even get extended. Louise swore she wanted to come back in two months, but I'd bet my retirement she decides to take her full leave."

Before Evolet could comment, the phone on Julie's desk rang. Julie bustled back around and picked it up.

"Yes?... Yes, she just arrived. I'll show her back."

She hung up, grabbed a leather folio off her desk and turned to Evolet with another big smile. "Mr. Bradford is in the conference room with representatives from another company. He'd like you to join them there."

Evolet frowned. "I was told I'd be working for Ms. Roberts."

"Oh, there must have been a misunderstanding." Julie gestured for Evolet to follow her down the hall. "Ms. Roberts put the call in to the agency for a temporary executive assistant, but it was for Mr. Bradford. She's worked with them before, so Mr. Bradford asked her to reach out personally and find someone who had your experience."

Momentarily unsettled, Evolet glanced out the window. She preferred to be prepared going into a new job. An online search of her new employer was a must and, if she had time, a quick check-in with the group chat the temp agency maintained to see if anyone else had worked for the company before.

Couldn't be helped. But who, she wondered, was Mr. Bradford? Some intimidating billionaire who would bark out orders? Or someone spoiled with a lack of focus, someone who would expect her to do most of the heavy lifting?

"Is everything all right, dear?"

Evolet turned and smiled reassuringly at Julie. "Yes. I thought I was working for Ms. Roberts," she confided to ease some of the concern in Julie's eyes, "so I did some snooping on her online profile this morning. I like to know a little about who I'm working for and their interests." She smiled again in reassurance. "I don't like going in unprepared, but I'll manage."

"Well, I can tell you all you need to know about Edward Bradford," Julie said as her heels clicked against the wood floor. "He likes to portray himself as stodgy and unreachable, but we're very fortunate to have him leading us. Very intelligent, just like his father, and doesn't mind getting his hands dirty. I've seen him work the assembly line at his manufacturing plants to understand what his workers are going through. You don't get many *Fortune* 500 CEOs doing that," Julie added proudly as they neared a wide doorway.

Reassured by Julie's staunch defense of her boss, Evolet relaxed. It was just eight weeks. She'd worked for a variety of bosses—some friendly and engaging, some distant and even downright rude. Just because this was the most profitable and esteemed company she'd worked for didn't mean anything in the long run for her ultimate career goals.

Just a means to an end, she reminded herself.

Her eyes widened as she spied the last door at the end of the hall just past a flight of stairs that hugged the wall. Covered in tufted burgundy leather with gleaming brass buttons, the door stretched nearly to the ceiling.

"A beauty, isn't it?" Julie said with pride. She paused and gestured toward the door. "Edward's father had it in his office. When we moved here, Edward had the door installed." Her smile turned sad. "David would have appreciated that. We don't talk much about him, but Edward loved him very much."

"You worked for Edward's father, then?" Evolet asked gently.

"And David's father."

"His father?" she repeated. "But…you…" At the

humorous gleam in Julie's eyes, she plowed ahead. "You don't look old enough to have worked that long."

Julie's laughter echoed down the hall. She reminded Evolet of Constanza, happiness and contentment radiating off her small frame in palpable waves that couldn't help but make one smile.

"That is a wonderful way to start off a Monday. I think you're going to do just fine here at Bradford Global, Evolet Grey."

She resumed walking and turned into an open office space. People lounged on leather couches, sat around low-slung coffee tables scribbling on tablets and typed away at state-of-the-art computers at one of the many desks artfully arranged in the giant room. More of the black iron chandeliers hung from a soaring ceiling. The black-and-white photographs on the navy brick walls made Evolet feel like she'd been shoved back in time to the industrial era. A blend of past and present.

Her esteem for Edward Bradford rose. She'd seen enough bland office settings with cubicles that encouraged solitary work and little to no social interaction. Bradford seemed to have gone in the opposite direction, with a coffee bar in the corner and a balcony just beyond filled with sumptuous outdoor couches and chairs.

Julie called out a few greetings as she led Evolet toward a staircase that hugged the bricks and led up to a glass-enclosed room. Evolet responded to the curious glances with a smile. She liked getting to know the people she worked with on her assignments, chatting with them in the break room and making small talk. But the benefit of being a temp was just that—she was temporary. It was easy to brush off overtures of friendship because in a matter of days, weeks or even occasionally months, she would be gone. No need to get her hopes up or to have the threat of losing someone she started to care about looming over her head.

The interior of the glass room came into view. The glass was broken up by thick black beams, beyond which sat several men and women around a large conference table having what appeared to be a heated discussion.

"What was that?" Evolet asked as Julie murmured something under her breath.

"Titan Manufacturing," the older woman responded. Perhaps Evolet was reading too much into Julie's tone, but she didn't sound like she was a fan. "They didn't move past the first round of bidding for the Royal Air contract, and now they're trying to…encourage us to partner up for the final round." She turned and handed Evolet the leather folio. "There's a tablet in there for taking notes. Please note any details about any proposals so Mr. Bradford can review it later. There's a chair and a small table at the back where you can sit. Mr. Bradford will meet with you in his office afterward to go over the details for the next few weeks." Her sunny smile returned as she laid her hand on the door handle. "Welcome to Bradford Global, Miss Grey."

Just like before she went onstage, butterflies rushed through Evolet's stomach. And then they were gone, replaced by determination and an iron will to succeed.

"Thank you."

The door opened. An angry voice rolled out, vibrating with desperation. "You undermined us in the first round of bidding, Bradford! The least you can do is bring us on."

"You undermined yourself, Thad. Don't blame us for your company's shortcomings."

The familiar deep voice rolled over Evolet's skin like a lover's caress. The air grew heavy as her breathing quickened. Her head jerked to the right.

And there he was. Larger-than-life as he sat at the end of the conference table, his broad shoulders clad in a charcoal-gray suit that simultaneously seemed tailor-made for him and yet barely contained the muscles that rippled beneath the wool. He leaned back in his chair, one hand on the table, the other hanging casually at his side.

But she knew better. Her heartbeat quickened until it was pounding so wildly in her chest she couldn't believe the sound didn't rise above the near shouting. She saw the sharp edge in his gaze, the restrained temper in the cords of muscle in his neck.

Her eyes flicked to the still-arguing man with thick black hair and artificially golden skin. A man, she decided, who didn't notice details, like when he was in the crosshairs of a much more powerful predator.

Damon's gaze slid to hers. Did she imagine the flare of surprise, the slip of control? She blinked, and all she saw was the calm mask he'd worn when he'd dismissed her on the dance floor. Cool, competent and unapproachable.

The initial stab of hurt at seeing how unaffected he was disappeared, replaced by questions like why he had given a false name. Was it something as simple as a nickname? Or something more scheming?

Resolution and determination took hold. It didn't matter. He'd had his reasons, and they were none of her concern. She turned her back on him and walked to the chair. She couldn't work for the man she'd so shamelessly kissed in Central Park. But she was still a professional. She would finish the meeting, take notes and then speak with him afterward to formally resign. Her nose wrinkled at the thought of calling her agency. She'd worked for them long enough, and certainly earned them enough money, that they would be kind. But she'd never walked away from a job before. She would owe them an explanation.

Because I wrapped myself around the CEO of Bradford Global like a python as he kissed me senseless?

She bit back a snort of laughter. The humor wiped away the last traces of shock and cemented her control over the moment. She removed her coat with quick, methodical movements, took the tablet out of the folio and sat.

Damon's attention was still focused on the man with the artificial tan. She took one last look, allowed herself one more indulgence of remembering the way his fingers had grazed her cheek, the way he'd held her as if he couldn't get enough of her...and then slipped into her role as Evolet Grey, temporary executive assistant to the CEO of Bradford Global, as she banished her feelings for the man she'd kissed in the rain.

CHAPTER FIVE

IT HAD, Damon decided as he walked down the hall toward his office with Evie or Evolet or whatever she called herself walking behind him, been the longest meeting of his life. Given the number of meetings he'd sat through, that was saying something. The more Thad Williams from Titan Manufacturing had argued, the more Damon had entertained fantasies of having security summoned to haul the man out by his designer paisley tie.

Better to indulge in that fantasy than ones centering on the woman who'd sat calmly in the back of the conference room throughout the entire circus.

Evolet Grey, his temporary executive assistant for the next two months.

He had barely survived one meeting. How could he survive eight weeks with her in his building, his meetings, *his office*?

When he had looked up to see her standing in the doorway, staring at him as if she'd seen a ghost, he'd pressed his feet into the floor to mentally anchor himself so he didn't go to her. Never had the sight of a woman with her hair bound at the base of her neck and a billowing trench coat aroused him so much.

Never, either, had the sight of a woman distracted him from a meeting. That thought had been enough to pull him back from his memories of Friday night to focus on the people seated around the table. It was also enough for him to know that, once they reached his office, he would need to dismiss her.

He pushed the door open, the feel of the cool leather a sharp contrast to how hot he felt. Good God, he had *kissed* the woman. A simple kiss that had slid like a drug through his veins and left him wanting as he'd never wanted before.

"Come in," he said over his shoulder when he didn't hear her follow him in. "And shut the door." His eyebrows rose as he heard her mumble something. He circled around his desk. "What was that?"

She looked at him then. How had he thought her cool and reserved at the fundraiser? He must have been blind because now that he saw the banked temper simmering in her eyes, he couldn't see her as anything but fire and passion seething beneath the surface.

"I said, 'Are you sure that's a good idea, sir?'"

A shudder passed through him at her proper tone, the primness failing to cover the underlying sass.

"Why wouldn't it be? We're both professionals. Unless," he added with a mocking smile, "you're concerned you won't be able to control yourself."

A flush crept up her neck and over her cheeks. Her eyes glittered as her lips thinned. He returned her stare, keeping his face smooth even as his eyes devoured the sight of her. Her bun was still perfect, every hair smoothed into place. It didn't erase the memory of the golden strands wound between his fingers as he had claimed everything she had offered with a ruthless need that had only grown after she'd fled into the storm.

Now, with her standing before him, dressed in a billowing white blouse with a prim tie at her throat and black pants, the perfect professional, his need was almost ferocious.

All the more reason to dismiss her. She would be a distraction, one he couldn't afford right now. That and he didn't care for the strength of his fascination. He had no doubt that sex with Evolet Grey would be one of the most pleasurable experiences of his life. But he also suspected that it would involve giving more than he had ever given before to another woman. Giving meant surrendering control.

No infatuation would ever take precedent over staying in control.

He gestured for her to take a seat, waiting until she sat before he sat behind his desk. "I'm glad to see you made it home safe."

"Thank you," she replied stiffly. She glanced around the office. "Not bad for Edward Bradford, the CEO of Bradford Global. Or is it Damon? I wasn't aware CEOs used aliases these days."

Irritated, he leaned forward and steepled his fingers. "Thank you, *Evie*."

She had the good grace to flush. "It is my name," she said defiantly, and damned if that pert tone didn't make him hard.

"Just as Damon is mine." When she frowned at him, he shrugged. "Edward Charles Damon Bradford."

"Middle name," she grumbled. "Why didn't you tell me who you were?"

"I enjoyed being anonymous. It's rare to find someone who doesn't know who I am, what I do and the estimated number of zeroes in my bank account."

"Rather presumptuous to think I'd be dazzled by four names and a fancy office."

He couldn't help himself. He grinned. "Most people are impressed when they learn who I am and what I do."

"I'm not most people, am I?"

"No," he said, suddenly serious. "You're not."

She blinked, some of her bravado slipping as she looked at him with an almost confused expression on her face. Her gaze slid away from his. Silence descended, along with the pressing weight of what he had to do next.

But before they dealt with the uncomfortable business of having her reassigned, he held out his hand. "The tablet, please, and your notes."

She handed over the leather folio. He opened the folder and leaned back, his eyes scanning the screen. The more he read, the more a headache started to pound at his temples. It was easy to see why the temp agency Laura had contacted had recommended Evolet.

She was good. She was very, very good. Not only had she taken detailed notes, she'd also kept a separate column where she'd transcribed some of the conversations taking place around the table while Thad had monologued at Damon.

"Brigid LaRue is considering quitting Titan Manufacturing?"

"She is." Evolet's lips twitched. "Mr. Williams has little interest, or respect, for her ideas."

His mind conjured up an image of Titan's head of

marketing, a svelte woman whose olive green suit had complemented her brown skin and black hair braided into a thick bun. She'd been polite yet assertive, managing to slide in a couple pitches between Thad's rants that, even though Damon had no interest in a partnership with Titan, had been impressive.

"How did you hear all this?"

She shrugged. "Many people don't think of executive assistants. And when they do, it's because they need a cup of coffee or a new pen. They talk around us like we're not even there."

Damon frowned. "Then you've been working for the wrong people."

Her eyes narrowed. "This isn't my career, Mr. Bradford. It pays the bills until I join a professional orchestra."

"You're very good at it."

"And you're good at dancing, but I assume you're not pursuing professional ballroom dancing anytime soon." Her smile took the sting out of her words. "I like what I do for NYC Executives. I like the details, the organization, the dependability." She hesitated on the last word, as if she'd revealed more than she had wanted, but continued. "I'm fortunate that I have something I like while I pursue what I love."

He regarded her for a moment with a thoughtful stare before glancing down at the document Julie had printed for him that morning—Evolet's résumé from the agency, which included relevant positions she'd held. He'd been both relieved and energized by her experience given that he had been depending on Louise still being here through the submission of the final proposal to Royal Air. He'd reviewed the résumé before the meeting with Titan, before he'd known Evolet Grey was the same woman whose lips he had plundered and body he had claimed without a single article of clothing shed.

His gaze slid back up to her. He steeled his body against the initial rush of desire, battled it back with reason and the knowledge that it would be very hard to find someone of Evolet's capabilities and knowledge. Not in time for the next stage of the Royal Air contract.

She was beautiful. She was intriguing. But she was a temporary existence in his life. Nothing mattered more than Bradford Global and seeing the company succeed. He could contain his libido for the duration of Evolet's contract. His fascination with her would fade with time and doing what he did best—throwing himself into work. It had been the cure for more than one emotional ailment in the past. It would work again.

The white of her blouse made her blush all the more noticeable as it crept up her neck.

"Well…" She cleared her throat. "On that note, I will notify the agency that this won't work and I—"

"Why won't it?"

Her eyes widened to an almost comical size, large and gold, emotions flashing through them without concealment or artifice.

"Did your agency brief you on the project Bradford Global is bidding on?"

Suspicion lingered on her face, but she nodded. "Royal Air. They're adding to their fleet and need a reputable manufacturer who can produce planes under a tight deadline."

Damon nodded, pleased. "Bradford Global is one of the three companies in the final running for the contract."

Interest sparked in Evolet's eyes. "Congratulations."

The sincerity in her voice warmed him. He inclined his head.

"Thank you." He gestured to the résumé on his desk. "You worked five months as an executive assistant for a CFO for a major US airline and four months for the head of marketing for another. You have over six years of experience in this type of work. Past employers have remarked on your diligence, talent for details and 'pleasant manner,'" he added with a coy look in her direction. "When Laura called the temp agency, you were their first recommendation."

"And I appreciate that, but…" Her voice trailed off as her blush deepened. "What about…well, the… thing?" she finished weakly.

"Thing?" he repeated casually.

She rolled her eyes. "You kissing me in Central Park."

"As I recall, you kissed me back. Yet so far, we've managed to exist for—" he glanced at his watch "—eight minutes in the privacy of my office without a repeat performance." He arched a brow, ready to deal his final card. "Unless you think you can't keep your hands off me."

Bull's-eye.

Her eyes hardened as she sat up straight. "Of course I can. It was just a kiss."

It was exactly the attitude he needed her to have to make this working relationship successful. The little stab of irritation that she could deem what had happened between them as "just a kiss" was inconsequential.

"Good. In that case, Miss Grey," he said with a sharp smile, "let's get to work."

CHAPTER SIX

EVOLET'S FINGERS DRUMMED a steady beat on the handle of her cello case as the elevator soared upward. Hauling the instrument on the subway was less than fun in the early morning rush, but it was worth it to have the extra practice time. The first couple of days, rushing home on the subway, getting her cello and making the walk to Central Park, had left her with precious little time to practice. By Wednesday, she'd taken to bringing her cello with her and hopping off at the Fifty-Ninth Street station and practicing in the park. With her audition for the East Coast Chamber Orchestra later in the week, she needed all the practice she could get.

Excitement hummed inside her. It was her first audition in over a month. Not her dream position, but a respected and growing orchestra that would be a good first step into the world of playing professionally.

But that was later, Evolet reminded herself as she exited the elevator. Right now, Bradford Global commanded her focus. It had been two weeks since she'd joined the company. Two weeks that had dragged on and flown by in equal measure. No matter how early she arrived, she had not yet beaten Damon to the office. They started off with an overview of what the day would look like, from touring the existing manufacturing facilities to reviewing pieces of the reports filtering in from various departments that would be submitted to Royal Air. Dizzying amounts of information, hours spent poring over documents.

And the man who starred in what was turning into nightly erotic fantasies often just a few feet away from where she worked.

She had an office, a beautiful room with a large window that overlooked the Brooklyn Bridge and the blue waters of the East River. At first, she had resisted adding any homey touches. She was a temporary worker, not an employee. She'd spent months at other companies and never once felt the inclination to personalize whatever space she was assigned.

But there was something different about Bradford Global. Amazing, she thought as she stepped off the elevator and waved to Julie, what working for a company that invested in their employees could do. It wasn't just the perks, like the coffee bar in the cavernous workroom she'd passed on her first day or the catered luncheons. It was the genuine friendliness Julie greeted every employee with, how Damon knew the names of everyone who came into his office and remembered to ask about their children, their college studies, their dog. His other executives, like Laura Roberts, mirrored his attitude of respect.

The first time she had been invited out for after-hours drinks with a group of engineers and assistants, she'd been so startled she'd said yes. She'd silently cursed herself all the way to the bar, only to stay two hours and find herself relaxing, enjoying conversation with people who were quickly turning from strangers to casual acquaintances.

A thought that would have made her uneasy just a short time ago. Instead, it had made her look forward to her days at the office.

Another red flag. She had fallen into her job with NYC Executives when she'd been attending college. It had offered flexibility and, best of all, temporary placements. No time to get attached to people, a job, if she moved every few weeks to months. She preferred no attachments.

Then why, she groused at herself as she walked down the hallway to her office, *am I getting involved?*

She'd turned down the second invitation for another night out with an excuse of needing to practice. But the third invite—a group dinner at an Italian restaurant that served savory pastas and bruschetta topped with tomatoes and fat slices of mozzarella—had resulted in her staying for three hours, sipping on wine and laughing as her coworkers had debated current events and swapped stories.

They'd even asked about her music—questions that had both surprised and touched her.

She was getting involved. She needed to stop.

A text lit up her phone as she walked into her office and set her bag on her desk next to the photo she'd put up of her, Constanza and Constanza's son, Samuel. She laid her cello case down in the corner.

"Hey, did you get my text?"

Evolet looked up with a smile to see Audrey Clark, one of Bradford's marketing pros, standing in the doorway. She reminded Evolet of Julie, her thousand-watt smile a flash of white against smooth dark skin. The two had connected over drinks that first night, chatting about everything from Audrey's father's playing for a jazz band in his retirement to their mutual interest in murder mysteries.

"My phone just dinged," Evolet replied with a laugh.

"We're all going to a dance club Saturday night in the West Village. Want to join?"

Yes. Evolet stomped down her initial reply.

"Um…can I let you know? I'm not sure what all I have to do for work, and I've got an audition coming up for the East Coast Chamber Orchestra. I really need to practice."

"Whoa. I heard them perform at Bryant Park last summer. You must be excited!"

Guilt spurted through her. She knew the material for her audition backward and forward. As much as the extra practice boosted her confidence, one night out wouldn't doom her audition. But she couldn't get used to this camaraderie, didn't want to want the connections she was reluctantly but steadily forming with others.

"Don't congratulate me too soon. I haven't had a successful audition since I made it on to the Apprentice Symphony."

"Hey," Audrey said as she came forward and enveloped Evolet in a hug, "don't sell yourself short. How many people apply and don't even get an audition?"

Evolet stood frozen for a moment before she indulged in hugging Audrey back. Constanza had hugged her all the time. But other than that, physical touch had been in short supply during her life.

"Thank you, Audrey," she whispered.

"You're welcome. And I get it. Maybe next weekend."

"Everything okay?"

Evolet stiffened as Damon's voice washed over her. He stood framed in her doorway, devastatingly handsome in a three-piece charcoal suit and black tie. She'd never thought about waistcoats, much less how sexy they would look molded perfectly to a muscular chest and tapered waist, but she certainly did now.

She wrenched her gaze away before Audrey picked up on the sudden tension humming in the air.

"Yes. Audrey was just congratulating me on securing an audition."

"That is cause for congratulations."

"Thank you."

Damon glanced down at his watch. "Evolet, if you could report to my office in fifteen minutes, we've had some updates from our public relations department."

"Yes, sir."

He leveled an enigmatic gaze at her before disappearing down the hall.

"Sir?" Audrey said with a laugh. "I don't think anyone has called him 'sir' in years."

Evolet tried to shrug off the sensual energy clinging to her like a second skin. "He's my boss."

"Technically your agency is your boss. But regardless, it is okay to call him Damon. It takes a little getting used to, but once you do, he seems more accessible, less scary."

But she couldn't. The last time she had called Damon by his name, it had been moaning it, begging him not to stop seducing her with kisses in the middle of a spring storm.

"I don't know if anything could make him less scary."

Audrey frowned. "Has he done something to make you uncomfortable?"

Her guilt doubled. Damon had been nothing but a gentleman since she'd started working. That was probably part of what set her on edge. He tempted her with his very presence, whereas he continued to type away at his computer, field numerous phone calls or host meetings without a single glance in her direction.

"No. He's been great." She shrugged, trying to appear nonchalant. "It's me. He just seems…larger-than-life, I guess. The bachelor billionaire in the fancy office."

Audrey's laugh echoed down the hall as she headed out. "I would pay to see you say that to his face directly."

Evolet managed to answer a few emails, grab cups of coffee for both her and Damon, and make it into his office one minute before the deadline.

He didn't look up as she walked in, but he did spare a glance at the coffee cup she set on his desk.

"Colombian, black," she said as she sat in the chair across from him.

"Thank you."

She couldn't decipher the enigmatic gaze he slanted at her and instead chose to ignore it. "What do we have on the agenda today?"

"The two case studies I requested are back. We need to review them for accuracy, ensure the circumstances of the projects align with Royal Air's expectations and, if they're up to standard, incorporate them into the final bid document." He glanced down at his watch. "I have meetings at eight thirty, ten, one and four. You'll need to continue to review them while I'm away."

"Yes, sir."

He shot her another look. "You're doing that to annoy me."

Yes. It gave her a perverse pleasure to see something rattle that calm exterior and creep under his skin, especially something as innocuous as refusing to use his name. Only fair given that he'd left her tied up in knots for the past two weeks.

"What?"

He regarded her with a stare that at first amused her. But the longer he looked, the more she had to resist the urge to squirm as little tendrils of arousal wound their way over her skin. It wouldn't be so bad, she assured herself, if he wasn't so handsome, dark eyes set in that sharp, angular face that promised danger and charm.

"Are you happy here, Evolet?"

Surprised, she blinked and broke the seductive spell he'd woven with a single glance. "Happy?"

"Yes. Happy."

She tilted her head. "As happy as a temporary employee can be, I suppose."

"The staff speak very highly of you."

Pleasure warmed her before she squelched it. She liked Audrey, Julie, the people who had welcomed her with open arms.

But it shouldn't matter. Couldn't matter.

"You have a great team."

"Do you actually have an audition, or were you just deflecting Audrey's invitation?"

It took a moment for the full impact of his question to hit her. When it did, anger made her jaw clench and her fingers tighten on her tablet.

"Yes," she replied through gritted teeth. "I have an

audition." She pulled out her phone and with a few taps forwarded her audition notice to his email. "I don't lie, Mr. Bradford."

His computer pinged, but he didn't even glance at it, keeping her pinned with that emerald gaze that saw far too much.

"You don't owe me any explanations, Evolet. However," he continued as she started to speak, "I am curious as to why you hold yourself back when the team here at Bradford Global is not only willing but wanting to socialize with you."

She felt her mask slip, knew he saw that there was more to her antisocial attitude than mere shyness or introversion.

"It's eight twenty, Mr. Bradford. You should head up to your meeting."

His fingers tapped on his desk once, twice. And then he stood without another word, gathered his laptop and walked out the door.

She silently cursed. They'd made it two weeks keeping things professional. He didn't ask about her music. She didn't ask how he spent his evenings. That she spent any time imagining him dining at luxurious restaurants with beautiful dates dripping in diamonds or hosting elegant parties in a penthouse suite annoyed her immensely.

Focus.

If she hadn't experienced the hottest kiss of her life with her temporary boss, she would be thoroughly enjoying her job. Not only did she like the people, her office and the environment, but working on the bid for Royal Air was proving to be an enjoyable challenge. The bonus Bradford Global had added to her usual fee would allow her to take a couple months off after if she wanted. She could fill her days with music, creating content for the social media channels she maintained for her playing, and booking private events.

Her fingers drummed an impatient rhythm on the desk. It would be heaven at first. But, assuming she didn't get the position with St. John's, the Apprentice Symphony would be starting its summer break about the time her contract with Bradford Global was up. She didn't have anyone else in her life except Constanza and the occasional family outing with Constanza's son, Samuel. For so long, that had been enough.

When had she started wanting more?

Irritated, she stood up and walked down the hallway toward what was affectionately called the War Room, the massive open office space she'd passed on her first day that included the coffee bar exclusively for the use of Bradford Global's employees. A little coffee, a minute out on the outdoor balcony to take some deep breaths and center herself and then she'd get to work.

A smile crossed her face as she saw Julie at the bar. "Hi, Julie."

"Oh, hi, darling. How's it going?" Julie asked as she accepted a cup from the barista.

"Busy but good."

"I figured when I saw how late Damon's been staying."

Evolet frowned. "What?"

"The past two weeks, I don't think he's left his office before eight o'clock. I'm gone by five, but I review the security log every morning." She glanced down at her watch. "Speaking of time, I need to get back to my desk. Let me know if you need anything."

Evolet nodded absently as Julie walked off. Guilt niggled at her as she walked back to Damon's office, a latte in one hand and a biscotti in the other. The deadline was next week. Submitting on time was imperative. Submitting early was even better. She'd allowed her own preoccupation with their kiss to shadow her interactions with him, assume the worst when he appeared to be doing exactly what he'd said he would do and act in a respectful manner.

This was what came from letting emotions creep in, especially in business. She had let herself get distracted and missed the signs that her boss and the company she was working for needed a little more than she was giving. Time to mirror Damon's professionalism, stop acting like a moody teenager and do her job.

With her self-reproaching lecture over with, she sat down and began to work.

CHAPTER SEVEN

DAMON GLANCED DOWN at his watch and stifled a groan.
His four o'clock meeting had started twenty minutes
late and gone an hour longer than expected. Every time
he'd spied Evolet throughout the day, she'd been working even harder than she had been the last two weeks.
He had no doubt that a rough draft of the proposal,
including the case studies, would be ready for his review. He wanted nothing more than to shove it aside,
go home and relax on his balcony with a glass of bour-
bon and watch the sun set over the skyline.

Maybe next month.

Although the fact that he was wanting to leave before a project was completed unsettled him. For years
Bradford Global had driven nearly his every action. He
hadn't been able to, nor wanted, to relax if he had
unfinished business. Given the continuing expansion
and repeat business of satisfied clients, he almost always had something to do.

Perhaps it had been coming home to an empty apartment after he and Natalie had broken up. He didn't miss
her. But walking into the empty penthouse, everything
exactly as he'd left it, had begun to weigh on him.

Casual dates here and there suited him. Relationships were off the table. Maybe he should listen to Julie's advice and get a dog.

Evolet's face flashed in his mind. That was one entanglement he didn't need. Bad enough that he had kissed an employee like a starving man who'd just been granted his first meal in months. Worse was how she managed to do her job, do it well and not once look at him with the fire he'd glimpsed in her eyes in Central Park.

Never before had he been on the receiving end of an uninterested party. As arrogant as it sounded, women wanted to be with him, whether it was for sex, money, prestige or the occasional one who had professed to care about him. To have the one woman who had sparked his arousal for the first time in months—and to a degree he had never before experienced—treat him with cool professionalism grated on his usually steady nerves. It should have been impressive. Yet it almost seemed like she'd withdrawn into herself, become a milder, more placid version.

Once in a while, he caught a glimpse of the vivid spitfire he'd encountered at the gala, like her addressing him as "sir." From the tiny gleam of mischief in her eyes to the pertness in her voice, it had made him hard almost instantly.

Stop.

He needed to get a grip on himself. Not only was Evolet off-limits as his employee, but she had literally run away from him in the park. Whatever twist of fate had brought her to his company's doorsteps, he needed to focus on the positives of having someone with her experience and skill working on the Royal Air contract rather than this borderline obsession.

A rich scent teased his nose as he neared his office. Spices, meat, roasted vegetables. He hadn't eaten since lunch, and that had only been because Evolet had handed him a smoothie from the coffee bar in between meetings. Perhaps Julie had left him something, he thought with a fond smile. The woman had been a secretary for Bradford Global for over forty years, and she had treated all three CEOs like they were her children instead of executives over a multibillion-dollar company.

He opened the door to his office. And stopped.

Evolet was seated in one of the leather chairs, hair pulled up into a loose knot on top of her head, a few stray tendrils laying on her neck. He tightened his fingers into fists, a physical reminder to keep his hands to himself and not brush the hair off her neck before laying a kiss on her skin.

His eyes dropped down. Her legs were curled up underneath her, her bare feet peeking out from beneath the hem of her wine-colored dress. With a full skirt and sleeves down to her elbows, she should have looked matronly. Not sexy.

"What are you doing here?"

His frustration with the direction of his own thoughts made his voice snap out. Her head jerked up, her eyes widening at his tone.

"Um…working?"

He inhaled sharply and steadied himself as he walked to his desk. "You didn't have to stay late."

She shrugged. "Julie told me you'd been staying almost every night since I started. With the deadline next week, I wanted to make sure we would be ready in time."

He shot her an enigmatic smile that he hoped covered how oddly touched he was that she would be so invested in the work despite the temporary nature of her position. Then he spied two paper bags sitting on his desk. "What's this?"

"Dinner."

She set aside her laptop and sprang up. He watched, entranced, as she reached over with a soft smile and started pulling out containers.

"There's a Haitian restaurant on Beekman—Espwa. It's owned by a friend of Constanza's."

"Your adoptive mother."

She blinked up at him. "You remembered."

"I did. She's from Haiti?"

"Yes. Her father was Haitian. Her mother was from Puerto Rico. She came here after she lost her husband."

He watched, waited. She stared at him for a long moment before looking down at her food.

"My father died when I was three. I don't remember much, but he and my birth mother loved each other." Her lips turned down into a frown. "She didn't take his death well. I didn't have any other family, so I ended up in foster care when I was five. Bounced around for ten years until I landed with Constanza. She adopted me."

"I'm sorry."

"Nothing to be sorry about."

The casual shrug she gave him didn't distract him from the pain in her eyes, the slight bunching up of her shoulders, the nervous graze of her hand pushing a strand of hair out of her face.

"You lost both parents. I know what that's like."

Her head jerked up. His surprise at his own admission didn't stop him from holding her gaze. He wasn't sharing for himself. He was sharing to help her, an important distinction.

"Yes, I suppose you do."

"It hurts."

At last, she nodded.

"Very much. So does getting bounced around, never knowing where your next home will be."

"Does that have anything to do with your work for a temp agency?"

She speared him with an arched brow and a slight frown. "Is this an impromptu counseling session, or are we working?"

His lips curved up. "Do I make you nervous, Evolet?"

She held his gaze, as if to show him she could. But as they stared, he saw the change come over her, the rise and fall of her chest, the darkening of her eyes, the parting of her lips. She was the first to look away, with a casual toss of her head as she stabbed her fork into one of the takeout containers.

"No."

Oh, he was a selfish bastard, he thought with a satisfied smirk. He enjoyed hearing the slight hitch in her breath, seeing the tinge of pink in her cheeks. The woman might've been cool and competent in her work, but she still felt the attraction between them, wanted him just as he wanted her.

"Daniel's a fantastic chef. I rarely make it down to this part of the city, but when I decided to stay, I thought you might be hungry because I was hungry and…" She trailed off, then took a deep breath before she surprised him with a chagrined smile that was simultaneously stimulating and endearing. "I'm babbling. I'm nervous and I'm babbling."

There you are.

Here was the woman he'd danced with in a glamorous ballroom, whom he'd followed into Central Park and kissed in the rain. Here was the woman who, for a couple minutes her first morning here, had verbally sparred with and aroused him with her spunky attitude.

"Why are you nervous?"

She shot him a look that told him he was an idiot. "I stayed past my usual quitting time without talking to you and took over your office. It might seem presumptuous or…"

"No, no," he said with a delighted smirk as the pink in her cheeks turned to a red similar to the shade of her dress. "Or what?"

"Like I'm trying to set something up. You know, to…seduce you," she finally choked out.

He threw back his head and laughed. "If that's what you were trying to do, telling me ruins the effect somewhat."

She bit down on her lower lip, but he saw the corners of her mouth twitch up as she looked away.

"Then fortunately that wasn't my plan. I figured you might be hungry since you barely stopped to take a breath today. I hope you don't mind, but I ordered for you."

He ignored the slight reproach in her voice and inhaled as she pulled the lid off a large bowl.

"What is that?"

Unease furrowed her brow. "*Poulet aux noix.* It's spicy marinated chicken with bell peppers and cashews."

"It smells incredible."

Her face smoothed out into a relieved smile. "It

tastes even better. I also ordered *makawoni au graten* and *pikliz*. Haitian macaroni and cheese and a pickled vegetable relish."

"I've never had any of this."

"Then you're in for a treat. Sometime I'll have to get you their hot chocolate. You've never had hot chocolate until you've had Haitian hot chocolate."

She set the food out on his desk and pulled up a chair on the other side.

"Did Julie get you your company card?" he asked as he forked up a bite of noodles dripping with cheese.

"My card? For what?"

"Purchases like this."

She frowned. "No, she's just ordered whatever I needed. I took care of dinner."

He paused with the fork in midair. "You bought dinner?"

"Yes."

"I can have Julie—"

She held up a hand. "If you say *repay me*, I will dump this chicken in your lap."

He arched a brow. "That could be considered assault."

"Pummeled by poultry?" Her smile carried a hint of steel. "The bonus you're giving me is more than enough to buy dinner. I know you've been working late, and I admire that you don't ask anything of your employees that you're not willing to do yourself. I was hungry. It was a reasonable assumption you were hungry. So I bought us dinner. My treat."

That same warmth that had appeared when she'd told him she wanted the company to succeed intensified and spread throughout his body.

"I can't remember the last time someone bought me dinner. Thank you."

Another genuine smile flashed across her face. God, he wanted to see that smile in the mornings when he came into the office, not the tiny little twerk of her lips before her mouth settled into a straight, unexpressive line.

"You're welcome. You've been nothing but respectful while I've been here, despite our…history. I'm grateful you encouraged me to keep working here."

Grateful. The word erased the warmth and nearly destroyed his appetite. He didn't want her to be grateful. He didn't want her to make him feel like even more of a cad for entertaining thoughts of her naked and spread across the bed in his penthouse, arching against him the way she had in the park but this time with her breasts bared to his lips, his tongue…

He steeled himself against his lust. They had at least an hour ahead of them, if not more. He could keep himself under control for that long. Tonight, he'd cool off in a long, icy shower.

And tomorrow…tomorrow he would set up a date with someone, anyone this weekend to help get his mind off the entrancing woman currently sitting barefoot in his office eating macaroni and cheese.

"You're welcome, Evolet."

CHAPTER EIGHT

EVOLET GLANCED AT the clock and suppressed a yawn. Nearly eight o'clock. She could easily stay until midnight reviewing and editing the proposal.

But, she acknowledged with a satisfied wiggle in the leather chair she had settled into, they'd gotten a ton of work done. Once dinner had been eaten, they'd attacked different parts of the proposal and settled into a steady pace of work. They'd exchanged ideas, argued over the merits of one particular client testimony and honed the proposal into something she saw as the best project she'd ever worked on.

She glanced up. At some point Damon had taken off his jacket and rolled up his shirtsleeves, leaving him in his tie, waistcoat and shirt. It was decidedly unfair, she thought as she looked away, that even his forearms were muscled. For the most part, she'd kept to her resolutions to stay professional. But as he'd relaxed, the aloof air had evaporated, replaced by an intelligent man with a quick wit who challenged her ideas, encouraged her.

Why, she thought morosely as she stood and moved to the window, *couldn't he have just been nice to look at?*

The substance behind his handsome face made him all the more intriguing and attractive.

With a quick shake of her head, she looked out over the city. The sun had just dipped out of sight, leaving the horizon a painter's dream of magenta, pale orange and violet. Overhead the sky had slipped into darkness, deep blue serving as a backdrop for the proud skyscrapers of New York City jutting up toward the heavens. She'd never seen the city from so high up, historic landmarks sharing space with new creations, all of them lit with millions of golden lights that gleamed warmly in the late spring evening.

"Beautiful, isn't it?"

She started. Her eyes focused on his reflection in the glass just a few feet behind her.

"I don't know if I'd ever get any work done with a view like this."

"You get used to it after a while."

"How? How could something this incredible become mundane?"

He shoved his hands into his pockets, his expression darkening as he glanced between her and the city.

"That's a good question."

Something heavy lay beneath his words. She almost asked but stopped herself, remembering how quickly he had shut down when she'd inquired about his mother at the gala. They'd achieved a working harmony she didn't want to risk by asking nosy questions that were none of her business.

"I didn't realize how late it was."

"I didn't, either." She moved back toward the chair where she'd left her shoes. "But we got quite a bit done."

"What about your practice?"

Surprised, she looked up at him. "My practice?"

"You bring your cello with you to work almost every day. And," he added with a ghost of a smile, "Audrey told me you often stop and play in the park on your way home."

Evolet paused, suddenly shy. "The audition you heard me talking about with Audrey is for the Orchestra of St. John's. It's Thursday. Even though the Apprentice Symphony—the group I played with for the fundraiser—practices on Tuesdays, I try to play every day, and that's especially true if I have an audition coming up. I usually hop off at Fifty-Ninth Street, play in the park when the weather's nice so I don't bother my neighbors and then go home."

"What do you when it's raining or cold?"

"I use the church community room the Apprentice Symphony practices in." She glanced once more at the darkening sky. "But if I did that tonight, I probably wouldn't get home until after ten. I've practiced enough I'm pretty sure I play in my sleep."

"Still, you didn't have to stay. I know your music is important to you."

The way he said it, with genuine inflection, twisted her stomach into knots.

"Thank you. I feel pretty confident about the audition and, worst case, there will be another one later."

He tilted his head. "You don't sound that enthused."

Her hand came up, grasping for an explanation. "Is it bad that I'm almost more excited for the audition itself than the orchestra? It's a good orchestra, and I would be disappointed if I didn't make it."

"But not devastated."

"No," she replied with a smile. "Failing an audition

for the Emerald City Philharmonic, however, would be devastating. They were the first group I ever saw professionally in concert. Just getting a standard 'thanks for applying' email when I submitted my audition tape earlier this year was hard enough."

"That had to be hard."

"It was. But," she continued with determination, "I won't give up."

He returned her smile with one of his own that made her feel warm and feverish. "I've felt the same about contracts with other companies. I feel the same way about Royal Air as you do about Emerald City."

It wasn't just the physical attraction snapping between them, she realized, that electrified the air. It was a shared camaraderie, an understanding of the passions that drove them to achieve their goals.

Cold tendrils of fear stabbed through the warmth. Too much opening up. Too much vulnerability, especially with a man like Damon.

"It's getting late." Her smile morphed into a polite expression, one that hopefully clearly conveyed the personal confession portion of their evening was over. "We made a lot of progress tonight, and I want to be here on time tomorrow to wrap up the proposal."

"Would you like to practice before you go?"

She blinked. "Um, where?"

"Here. The office is soundproof."

"Ah, yes. Most CEOs I work with soundproof their office for the inevitable torturing of their employees."

It shouldn't have mattered so much to see humor flash in his eyes, see the ghost of a grin on his lips.

"When you deal with the kind of companies and money that I do on a regular basis, ensuring discretion and privacy is tantamount to keeping clients. Unless," he added with that same hint of potent masculinity he'd displayed when he'd all but dared her to work for him, "you don't want me to hear you play."

She scoffed. "You've already heard me play."

"In a crowded ballroom. Your solo was enchanting but only thirty seconds amid a slew of other performances. I would have thought playing for someone new might help you prepare for your audition. But if you're uncomfortable, I wouldn't want to push."

The hell you wouldn't.

Her chin came up. He shrugged, the grin turning into a full-blown, devilishly taunting smile. He was baiting her, and she knew it. But she couldn't let a challenge about her music pass by unheeded.

And unfortunately, he was right. Any type of practice in front of a new audience was good.

"I'll be right back."

Five minutes later she sat with her back to the city. As she tuned her cello, she could feel his eyes on her, hating the way her heart thudded against her ribs as a heated flush stole over her body. When she practiced with the Apprentice Symphony or performed at an audition, she was among other musicians, people who knew the craft as well and often better than she did. Her nerves in those circumstances were solely fixated on playing the right notes, achieving the right volume, harmonizing with her fellow musicians or accompanist.

But now, she felt naked, exposed to every sweep of Damon's gaze. She hadn't performed like this for anyone except Constanza in years. Even at her auditions, she always had an accompanist.

"You're stalling."

"How do you know?" she retorted.

He grinned. She shook her head, picked up her bow and began to play.

The bow sank into the strings, the vibration rippling through her body. Her eyes drifted shut as the music filled the room. Deep and somber, the notes blended together to tell a story of love and loss, of growing old and saying goodbye. She drifted into the music, her body swaying with the cello as she poured her own losses and grieving into the movements, each emotion made more potent by the glimpse of happiness she'd been given by the man sitting just a few feet away.

The music swelled into a crescendo, then drifted off into sorrow. She sat for a moment, taking in a deep breath as her body relaxed.

At last, she opened her eyes.

And nearly swallowed her tongue.

Damon watched her. Never had one gaze conveyed so much. He leaned back in his chair, the same deceptively casual stance he'd been in when she'd first glimpsed him in the ballroom. Just like that night, his eyes burned with an intensity that ensnared her, tempting her to release herself from the restrictions she'd placed on her heart.

"You play beautifully."

Huskier than normal, his voice wound about her like a seductive spell.

"Thank you."

"Do you always play sad songs?"

The question caught her off guard and eased some of the sexual tension building between them.

"No. I play a variety. There're quite a few videos on

my social media and a few on my website. Some are sad, some are happy, some are fun."

"Your solo at the gala was sad."

Her hand tightened on the cello's neck. "I was sad. So, I played something sad."

"Why were you sad, Evolet?"

If he hadn't said her name, she would have been able to resist. But the touch of the personal, the genuineness in his voice made her lips part.

"Constanza moved to an elder care facility across the river a couple years ago. She'd had a bad morning the day of the fundraiser. It's hard seeing her like that."

"Bad how?"

"Alzheimer's. She was diagnosed two years ago and is still in the early stages. But some days are worse than others." She looked out at the darkening sky. "That day she kept asking for Samuel and me. We were the only ones she could remember."

"Samuel?"

"Her son. The only biological child she had." She smiled wistfully. "But she fostered over one hundred children."

"And adopted you."

"Yes. She is my mother. The only one I've ever really had. I went to her home and played for her. The music usually calms her." She started to fiddle with one of the cello pegs. "And it did. Just hard to see her like that."

"You're doing it again."

Her head snapped up, her eyes narrowing. "Doing what?"

"Downplaying what happened. Like you did at the

fundraiser when you told me how you got started with the cello."

"I don't share my personal life with strangers."

Silence descended. She realized they were in some sort of emotionally charged standoff as their gazes held, tension building between them as they each waited for the other to look away. His hand rose, one finger lying casually on his cheek as the others curled into a fist and eclipsed his mouth from her view.

"Play another for me."

She blinked but didn't waver. It almost sounded like a command, one she would have normally refused simply on the principle of saying no to an order. To establish that just as his private life was off-limits to her, so was her past to him.

But, she realized as she nodded and brought the bow up, she wanted to play for him. She wasn't capable of fully sharing herself with anyone else. She'd done so with Constanza, would always be grateful for it. But Constanza's diagnosis, moving out of the apartment they'd shared for nine years and into the facility, seeing the one human being she had counted on since she was a teenager become a shadow of her former self had cemented that she would never allow another person into her life. Too many times she'd gotten her hopes up. Too many times she'd been left alone.

Playing was the closest she came to a relationship. That Damon had heard her solo amid the chaos of the fundraiser, picked up on the emotions swirling beneath the notes meant something to her.

Instead of dissecting why it meant anything—or why she was driven to share with him at all—she dragged the bow across the strings once more and descended into a poignant, haunting song dripping with unrequited desire. She'd played the song before, a dozen times. But playing it for Damon in the intimacy of his office, the memory of his kiss burning on her lips, she could feel the fervor in the harmonious blending of the notes, lust and longing crashing together in a scorching spiral that promised a night of passion unlike any other.

She had never understood the story behind the song, couldn't envision the emotions that were supposed to bleed from the sheet music into her playing.

But she did now. She'd never made love before, had never been tempted by the few dates she'd gone on. Lackluster kisses and groping hands had never inspired enough interest to take someone to her bed. Some of the women at the agency had encouraged her to try a dating app. Given that she barely had enough time for her music, her work to pay the bills and visiting Constanza regularly, she hadn't seen the point in going on potentially disastrous first dates in search of a fleeting sensation.

Yet as she cradled the cello between her thighs and thought of Damon, thought of his hands on her skin, his lips on hers, his harsh breathing echoing her own as they'd kissed in the rain, she knew that with someone like him, making love could truly be this chaotic, this wonderful.

She opened her eyes as she neared the end. Whether he had her in his web or she had him, she couldn't have torn herself away from meeting his stare. As he watched, his eyes devouring every movement of her fingers, the slide of her bow, the tilt of her body, she discovered it was possible to have the second most sensual experience of her life without a man ever laying a finger on her.

The song ended. Her body throbbed, deep beats that left her feeling heavy and unfulfilled. He maintained the same position he'd been in when she had started playing, his mouth hidden by his hand, his gaze focused on her. She knew he had been just as affected as she. But the fact that he remained so calm on the surface clawed at her pride.

"Satisfied?"

"Very."

He stood in one fluid motion, the elegance of the movement contrasted by his sheer masculinity. He crossed to her, and her breath caught in her chest as he reached down and lifted her hand, bow still in hand, to his lips.

"Thank you, Evolet."

The simple words sliced through her, cutting through her defenses and jabbing straight at her heart. Before she could summon a reply, he turned from her.

"Music has never been a focus of mine. But I've always been impressed by musicians and the talent it takes to play."

Conversation. He was making casual conversation, she realized dully.

"Um…with practice, it's not too hard." She forced herself to stay calm, to not succumb to her own desire, nor her rising anger, as she stood. "I maintain that anyone who has an interest can become a musician."

"I flunked piano lessons at the age of seven. Spectacularly enough that my parents never bothered to book me another tutor again."

She heard the smile in his voice. The simple glimpse

into his past cooled some of her irritation and stirred her sympathy. The one happy memory she had of her father was of a deep, booming laugh and being tossed up toward the sun on a warm summer day. The memories she had of her mother mostly involved a pale figure draped across a couch or passed out on the floor with an empty bottle nearby.

To have primarily good thoughts of one's parents, even in loss, was a gift most took for granted.

"Let me show you."

He turned back to her, his expression unreadable. "Excuse me?"

She gestured toward the empty chair. "I'll give you a quick lesson before I go."

"No."

She arched a brow. "Ah. That bad, huh?"

"My mother was an eternal optimist. Even she believed I was a lost cause."

"I think you're scared."

It was fun to have both the upper hand in finally unsettling him as much as he did her and causing a flicker of irritation to make his eyes narrow.

"I am not scared. Just practical."

"Sounds like a synonym for a scaredy-cat to me." She shrugged and started to reach for her case. "No matter. You're probably right. You would have played terribly."

He stalked across the room. She bit back a smile as he sat, his shoulders tense, his hands resting awkwardly on his knees.

"Five minutes. Show me."

"Not sure how much I can actually teach you in five minutes, but okay."

She helped him hold the cello and the bow, adjusting for his significantly larger height.

"I thought you didn't let anyone else touch your cello."

"I don't let anyone else carry my cello," she corrected him as she grasped his hand around the bow. "There's a world of difference between someone flinging it around like a duffel bag and teaching someone how to handle it respectfully. I give lessons in the park sometimes after I finish practicing."

"You teach?"

"Don't sound so surprised. I can be quite patient and charming when I wish."

He grumbled something under his breath.

"Come again?"

"Nothing. Now what do I do?"

"All right, make sure your thumb is in the center… good. You're going to drag the bow across the strings and use your elbow…"

She walked him through the steps. Each note he played made her inwardly wince even as she pasted an encouraging smile on her face. "Good."

"Liar."

She laughed. "A terrible one. Here…" She walked behind him and laid her hand over his. The warmth of his bare skin beneath her palm made her tense. "Lay the bow on the D string. And then pull with your elbow…"

A rich sound filled the air for a second.

"See! You can do it."

He glanced over his shoulder, one eyebrow arched in amusement. "I get credit for that?"

"You do."

Suddenly she realized just how close her lips were to his. One slight move and...

Stop! her rational mind screamed. *Don't be a fool!*

"Well," she said in what she hoped was a much cooler voice as she stood and moved away, "it's late."

He stood, gently laying her cello inside the open case, his back to her. She yanked her eyes away from his broad shoulders and moved to the window, wrapping her arms around her middle as if she could protect herself from this ridiculous attraction.

"It is."

She saw him appear once more in the glass. Even if she hadn't seen him, she would have felt him, that warm, rich scent that reminded her of spiced whiskey teasing her as he moved so close, she could feel the heat of his body on her back.

"Miss Grey..."

She closed her eyes at his formal address. How could he have missed her ridiculous reaction to him? Was he going to tell her to leave? Fire her?

"Evolet."

He gripped her shoulders and spun her around. One arm wrapped around her waist and dragged her against him, his body like steel beneath his clothes. The other hand slid up her neck, dislodging the loose knot and sending her hair cascading past her shoulders.

"Evolet," he said again, her name sounding like both a prayer and a curse on his lips, "if you don't want this—"

She surged forward, wrapping her arms around his neck and kissing him. He froze for a moment before his fingers tightened in her hair and he groaned. He anchored her head, plundered her mouth. Her breasts swelled against his chest. She wanted, so badly, to have his hands on her bare skin, to see him without the barriers of clothing.

As if he'd read her mind, he swept her into his arms and carried her over to his desk. He sat her on the edge and moved between her thighs with a confidence that stole her breath. His lips returned to hers, sending spiraling shoots of heat through her veins. One hand moved to her back, and she dimly heard the hiss of her zipper, felt the cool air kiss her back.

"Dear God," he whispered. "You're not wearing a bra."

Insecurity flitted across her senses, leached away some of the heat.

"I didn't not wear one on purpose. My, um, breasts aren't that big, and the dress has a built-in—"

"You're babbling again," he said with a smile that managed to be both wicked and carefree. It surprised her so much that she stopped talking long enough for him to lower his head and capture a nipple in his mouth.

Sensation exploded, spread like vines twining over her skin, binding her to the point of pleasure as his tongue swirled over her, teeth lightly scraping. Seeing his dark head against her breast sparked a carnality that drove her to the edge of her control. She teetered on the edge, wanting so much more, scared to take even a drop of what was being offered. If he could arouse her like this, with just a look, a kiss, a touch, what would happen if she were to fully surrender? Sex with Damon wouldn't just be sex. He would demand everything: heart, mind, body and soul.

His hands tightened on her waist. Her head fell

back, and he placed a soft kiss at the base of her neck where her pulse throbbed before trailing his lips down again. She let him push her gently down until she was stretched across his desk, her dress pulled down to her waist, her hair spreading out around her head.

With his hands and mouth working erotic magic on her skin, the ache she'd shoved away after their night together rising to the surface demanding relief, surrender suddenly didn't sound like a bad thing.

No, she thought as he kissed his way down her stomach, *it sounds like a very, very good thing*

Damon stood and gazed down at her with a possessive need that thrilled her to her toes. She smiled up at him.

He blinked. She started to reach for him, only to let her hands drop down as she watched him stare at her with hunger blazing in his eyes before he clenched his hands into fists and took a deliberate step back.

The full weight of all the rejections she'd experienced over the years came rushing back, eradicating her desire in one rush that stole the heat from her body and left her cold, draped half-naked across her boss's desk.

Damon turned away with a harsh oath. She closed her eyes, willing herself not to cry. Not in front of him. She wouldn't give him the satisfaction of letting him see how much he had affected her. How much he had hurt her.

How could she have thought him different? She sat up, lifting her bodice, the fabric feeling coarse against her skin as she slipped her arms into the sleeves. He was just like all the others, building up her hopes and making her think that maybe, just maybe, she needed to let go for a bit, start to let herself feel.

She slid off his desk and picked up her cello case without a backward glance. She would walk out of here with her head held high and email her boss at New York Executives letting them know she and Damon had had a disagreement and ask to be reassigned. She had never asked them for anything in seven years. They wouldn't like it, but they would do it.

She started for the door, her heart thudding dully in her chest, one hand wrapped around her cello case like it was a lifeline.

"Evolet."

She almost didn't stop. But something in his voice, the harsh darkness coating her name, made her stop.

When she looked back, it was to see him perched on the edge of his desk, one hand in his pants pocket, the other pinching the bridge of his nose.

"I'm sorry."

"Don't be," she said breezily in what she hoped was a voice that sounded like an experienced woman of the world and not a foolish virgin. "I'm sure I—"

"It wasn't you," he cut her off.

When he looked up, she nearly took a step back at the restrained passion that glowed in his eyes, a bright green fire that jump-started her heart back into a rapid dance that made her feel dizzy.

"I want you, Evolet. I want you, and I nearly took you right here on this desk."

Why didn't you?

She cleared her throat. "I noticed."

His choked laugh sounded anything but amused.

"I'm your boss, Evolet. Your boss. I've never kissed an employee, let alone started to make love to one."

"Technically I'm New York Executives' employee."

He waved her comment aside. "Don't make excuses for me or what happened here tonight. I owe you my profound apology for taking advantage of you like that."

Some of her earlier irritation started to return. "Funny, it seemed more like a joint effort to me."

"Whatever it was, it can't and won't happen again. I understand if you want to seek employment elsewhere."

Her mouth dropped open. "Are you firing me?"

"No. Just assuring you that if you choose to leave, I will make sure you have nothing but glowing references and the full amount for your contract with Bradford Global."

Her mind raced, his first words echoing in her mind.

I want you, Evolet. I want you, and I nearly took you...

An idea popped into her head. A completely mad, utterly ridiculous idea. But the more she examined it, the more it made sense. Not a decision to be made lightly nor in the heat of the moment.

But, she thought as she tilted her chin up, after a good night's sleep and a little more consideration, it might just be perfect.

"I didn't do anything here tonight I didn't want to. Now, if you'll excuse me, I need to get home and get some rest. I'll see you at eight tomorrow morning. Sir."

With that final petty but very satisfying snip, she walked out and gently closed the door behind her.

CHAPTER NINE

No MATTER HOW hard Damon focused on his computer screen, no matter how many times he reread the words, none of it stuck. His eyes kept darting to the clock, watching it tick closer and closer to eight.

What the hell had he been thinking last night? How could he have let himself lose control like that?

Too long without a lover had been one reason he'd conjured up at one in the morning when he'd lain awake staring at the ceiling. That damned song he'd encouraged her to play that had sounded like sex incarnate, another reason he'd grasped on to at four as he'd wandered into his kitchen and punched the power button on his coffee machine.

Or perhaps it was just that he couldn't get her out of his mind, which was what he'd finally settled on when he'd forced himself under an icy shower at five that morning. An experience that had been completely not worth the pain when he'd walked into his office and gotten hard just looking at his desk where Evolet had lain, golden hair spread across the surface, her body flushed a shade of pink that had looked all the more alluring against the contrast of her wine-colored dress yanked down to her waist.

When he'd pulled her dress down and uncovered her bare breasts, he'd nearly lost it then and there. The occasional shyness that cropped up, her embarrassment at appearing coquettish, had only added to her allure. The few times she let him see her—really see her— the contrasts of her personality intoxicated him. She could be calm and professional, analytical and perceptive. Their conversations last night—before he'd lost his mind—had stimulated him in a way no date had in a very long time. If ever.

But then she could be feisty, fire tempered by a compassionate nature he'd heard about from his employees and witnessed firsthand when she'd bought him dinner with her own money.

It shouldn't have mattered. But it did.

His computer dinged, and a notification signaled a new email. He clicked on it, his pulse ticking up. A calendar request for a meeting at eight o'clock from Evolet Grey.

She was probably going to quit. That or tell him she had filed charges against him for harassment. Nothing less than he deserved. Even if the emotional nuances of his attraction to Evolet weren't troubling enough, he had crossed a line.

The next nine minutes dragged on. Finally, the clock turned eight. His door opened not a second later, and Evolet walked in.

His chest tightened. Today she wore a black–and– white striped collared shirt and a pale yellow skirt with a black belt snug around her waist. Her hair was once more back in the severe bun. The memory of it spilling like silk over his wrists, caressing his skin as he'd kissed her, made his temper flare.

"Good morning, Evolet."

"Good morning. Is now a good time?"

With the resignation of a man heading to the gallows, he nodded. She crossed to the chair she'd occupied just hours before, curled up barefoot eating macaroni and cheese, and sat with the aplomb of a queen.

"I have two things to discuss with you—the first of which is the updated bid."

Business. He could handle business talk. He gestured for her to continue, and for eleven blissful minutes they reviewed the changes they'd made last night, discussed what work still needed to be done.

"Can we get the bid submitted before the thirteenth?" he asked.

"Yes. I would say at least a day before."

"Good."

Evolet cleared her throat. "Which brings me to the second matter I wanted to discuss with you."

Tension knotted his neck. "Yes?"

"Yes?"

Some of her bravado slipped. She breathed in deeply, her hands settling on her lap as she laced her fingers together. "I have a proposal for you."

"Interesting. Normally it's the man who does the proposing."

A blush stole over her cheeks. The sight of her skin turning pink tugged memories of the previous night to the forefront.

"Spit it out, Evolet," he growled.

"All right."

She looked him dead in the eye, and he suddenly

had the feeling that the world was about to drop out from under him.

"I want you to be my first lover."

There. I said it.

Evolet's triumphant thought was swiftly followed by panic.

Oh, God. I asked him to have sex with me.

She gripped her own hands tighter as she forced herself to sit and not run off like a scared little rabbit. The seconds ticked by, the tension ratcheting up with every passing moment.

And all Damon did was sit there, staring at her with an almost lazy air about him as if she hadn't just made the most indecent proposal of her life.

"Your first lover."

Finally, he spoke.

"Yes."

"As in…"

"I'm a virgin," she said impatiently.

"I see."

"After the contract is submitted. That takes precedent. Once the proposal is submitted, we can…" She waved a hand between them.

"Have sex."

"Yes." She smiled, pleased he was at least considering the possibility. "And then we go on our separate ways. I'll work at Bradford for the rest of my contract, and then we'll go on with our lives."

"Just like that?"

"Just like that."

Another long minute passed where she forced herself not to fidget. The more time passed, the more the weight of what she had just done settled on her shoulders, heavy and smothering. When she'd thought of it last night, she'd still been high on pleasure, desperate for him. Her solution had seemed like the perfect way to regain control, experience the thrills he had promised with his touch while adding an expiration date to their affair.

I want you, Evolet.

The raw yearning in his voice when he'd uttered those words had made her think that he would at least consider it.

But right now, sitting under his aloof, scrutinizing gaze, she felt like she had last night when she'd laid half-naked on top of his desk and he'd turned from her: Foolish. Ashamed. Rejected.

"Well, I guess that answers that." She stood and smoothed her hands across her skirt, the silky fabric calming some of her frayed nerves. "I'll make the same offer you made to me last night. If you're no longer comfortable with me serving in this role, I'll alert my boss and—"

"Why now?"

She blinked. "What?"

"Why, after twenty-five years of abstinence, are you looking to give up your virginity?"

"Because I've found someone I'm attracted to."

His brows drew together in a considering frown. "And you've never been attracted to anyone else before?"

"I have. But not like this." She shrugged, trying to appear nonchalant. "It's the twenty-first century. Women can ask men out, too."

He stood and circled around the desk, his face darkening into a thunderous expression. "There's a difference between asking a man out on a date and asking him to be the one to take your virginity."

The condescension in his tone sparked ire and embarrassment.

"Then forget I asked. I'll find someone else since you're not interested."

She started to turn away, but he moved quickly, coming up to her so fast she took several steps back until she bumped into the door.

"And how are you going to do that, Evolet? Post an ad online?"

"Not a bad idea," she fired back. "Do you think Click Here to Deflower a Virgin is too straightforward a title?"

One second they were standing nose to nose. The next he had placed his hands on either side of her head and leaned down until his mouth was so close she could feel his breath feathering across her lips.

"I didn't say no."

Warning whispered across the back of her neck as her skin prickled.

"So…is that a yes?"

"Where would this event take place?"

An image of the cramped apartment she'd lived in for the past ten years rose in her mind, her tiny bedroom barely big enough for a bed, her kitchen, living room and dining room all smooshed together in a space smaller than Damon's office.

"Um… I hadn't got that far."

"I'll pick the location, then."

Her heart sped up. "So that's a yes?"

"Are you comfortable continuing to work for me?"

"With you," she corrected. "Like I said last night, you're not my boss."

He made a noise that sounded almost like a growl. "Semantics."

"Not to me." She swallowed hard. "But I understand if the dynamic isn't one you're comfortable with. I could ask to be reassigned, or we could just not—"

He moved a fraction closer, cutting her off midsentence with his proximity.

"I'll respect your interpretation of our roles. But if at any point that changes, Evolet," he said, his voice turning harsh with emotion, "you tell me. Tell me, and I'll stop."

Touched, her hand came up before she could stop herself. Her palm settled on his cheek. He turned his head and pressed a heated kiss to her skin that made her gasp.

"Once the proposal is submitted, then."

Relief spiraled through her, followed by the intoxicating beat of anticipation mixed with desire. "Yes."

His gaze intensified. "Why me?"

"What?"

"Why me, Evolet?"

She started to make a joke, to pass it off as something not that important. But the way he looked at her, with something vulnerable flashing for a heartbeat, made her pause.

"Do you remember when we danced at the gala?"

"Vividly."

"You asked me to trust you." His eyes sharpened. "I did. It was the first time I trusted someone like that with my body in…ever. And you took care of me. I stumbled, and you caught me. We have something in-

tense and sexy between us, which is a bonus. But…".
She licked her lips. "I trust you. I want my first time
to be with someone I trust."

Finally, he moved. He kissed her, fierce and hot, before he pulled back and walked back to his desk. She
stood there, her back pressed against the door, her lips
swollen to the touch.

"A kiss to seal the deal."

His eyes flicked up, lust burning so hot she could
have sworn she would go up in flames on the spot. But
then she blinked and the man disappeared, replaced by
the distant CEO.

"We'll discuss details at a later date. But for now,
we have work to do."

CHAPTER TEN

EVOLET CHECKED HER email for the dozenth time since eight a.m.

"We submitted it ten minutes ago." The dry humor in Damon's voice made her look up. Amused, he nodded to her computer. "It'll probably be Monday at the earliest before we hear if Bengtsson wants any revisions and probably another week or two before he makes any decisions."

She sank back into her chair with a huff. "Did I mention I'm impatient?"

His eyes darkened before he refocused on his own computer. "I noticed."

She shot him a teasing look, but nervousness had her biting back a witty reply. Today she'd awakened with uneasy energy snapping in her veins. Today was the day they submitted the final bid, a full twelve hours before Royal Air's deadline. Part of the tension vibrating inside her like a taut wire was from what would come next. They'd shared the occasional heated glance or accidental brush of physical contact that made her breath catch, but there had been no more discussions, no more flirtations, no more searing kisses. There hadn't been time. It had been a whirlwind of a week as they'd reviewed the proposal over and over again—fine-tuning, discussing, meeting with others in the company, then revising again. It had been a heartening experience to see the level of investment from everyone in the company.

She wanted the contract for Bradford Global, and not just because she was besotted with the company's CEO. She'd continued to witness the work Damon's business did, where manufacturing quality equipment was just as high a priority as keeping its employees healthy and happy.

Perhaps, if the company her father had worked for had had the same attitude toward investing in its employees, the course of her life might have been very different.

"Where did you go?"

His voice slid into her musings, gentle and deep. It was odd to have someone she'd known less than a month become so in tune with her and her emotions. Once their deal had been struck, she'd felt the shackles she'd placed on her emotions loosen and start to fall away. The wanting that had been stoked in her the night of the gala had flared to life. She'd let Damon see more of her, the real her, than she had let anyone see in years, including herself. She didn't analyze everything she was going to say before it was said. She'd let herself relax and laugh at jokes, engage with the other employees.

It had also helped her realize just how utterly exhausting it had been to keep up those barriers between herself and the rest of the world. Even Constanza had commented on her last visit how much happier she'd seemed.

And she was. Mostly.

The audition with the Orchestra of St. John's had resulted in a brief email over the weekend thanking her for her time, saying the orchestra had gone in a different direction but she was always welcome to audition at a later date. It had hurt more than she'd liked, shaken her confidence. She'd spent hours in the park practicing, listening for what she had done wrong, analyzing every note until she'd been irritated and exhausted.

The sad truth was that there was a bevy of talented musicians and only so many spots. She could either give up or she could keep going. She'd indulged in a pity evening, including an old musical, popcorn and a long soak in her tub, then gone back out Sunday and played again.

Monday had brought another test. Damon had taken one look at her face and known something was wrong. Letting down her barriers had certainly let in more joy. But it had also brought with it an uncomfortable vulnerability she hadn't experienced since her early years in foster care. She could handle more friendships, more outings with coworkers, finally letting herself experience a physical relationship with a man whose company she enjoyed and who she found incredibly attractive.

Yet sharing her body felt safer than opening her heart. That she wanted to share more of herself every time he asked was a major red flag. But God help her, she wanted to be with him, to experience sensual pleasure with someone she liked, someone she trusted, someone who could make her entire body ache with a single glance.

Which is why, she reminded herself as she tucked a

loose tendril of hair behind her ear, *you came up with the arrangement.*

The terms were clear, finite. They would have sex. She would finish out her contract with Bradford Global. And then she would move on.

"I was thinking about how well you run your company," she finally said, finding a compromise on her thoughts. "I've never seen something run so smoothly or so strongly."

"Why did that make you sad?"

She tensed. "It didn't."

"Something did."

She looked up, ready to push back. The genuine interest and compassion in his eyes struck her, tugged at the strings she'd wrapped tightly around her heart. As a child, she'd rattled off her entire life story to the first two foster homes she'd stayed in. The families had been kind and considerate. One mom had listened to her and hugged her while she'd cried. Evolet had liked her a lot, had even started to envision staying with them and becoming a part of their family.

Only to have the system yank her out and place her in a new home three weeks before Christmas. She'd cried and begged to stay, but the family'd had the resources and training to care for a child with critical needs that many foster homes didn't. So Evolet had been transplanted to a home in a different school district.

Again and again, she'd gotten her hopes up, until finally one day she had woken up to the news that she was being transferred to yet another new house, another new school. Whether it had been the freezing cold hitting her in the face as she'd gotten off the bus or the sight of unfamiliar faces in a crowded school, she didn't know. All she knew was something had switched off inside her. Something only Constanza had managed to break through in the years since.

Until now.

Would it hurt anything? she wondered to herself.

Wasn't part of the reason she had propositioned Damon because there was something more than just attraction? Would sharing a small piece of herself be a bad thing?

"I was thinking about my father." She looked down at her teacup, fiddled with the string. "He worked as an electrician. Made good money, but if business was slow, things could get tight. The company he worked for cared more about getting things done than their employees."

She remembered his face the day he'd tossed her into the air, bright and vibrant. She also remembered it just a few months later, gray and wan, like someone had turned the light off behind his eyes.

"He worked an outside job in the cold. Got sick." She pulled the tea bag out, watched amber droplets fall and splash down into the cup. "Their equipment was old. He waited too long to go to the hospital because the company didn't provide health insurance. He didn't make it." She looked at him. "You make a difference, you know. The way you treat your people."

He watched her for a long moment, as if not sure what to make of what she'd just shared.

"Is that how you ended up in foster care?"

"I ended up in foster care because my biological mother preferred alcohol and pills over being a parent." She winced as the words came out, sharper and rawer than she had intended. "I was told she was a good mom before my father passed. I was only five when I went into care and don't have many memories before then."

He stood and moved to her, sitting down in the chair across from her. He leaned over, plucked the crumpled tea bag from her fingers and tossed it into the trash before sitting in front of her.

Why, she thought with sudden rising panic, *does this feel more intimate than kissing partially nude on his desk?*

"It's okay now," she said with a forced smile as she tried to discreetly scoot her chair back. "It's been years."

"Doesn't erase the pain."

She let out a breath. When she had shared pieces of herself with her foster families, they had always encouraged her to move on, to look to the future, to think about things that excited her. Never to grieve, to process what she had lost.

"No, it doesn't. Time lessens how much it hurts. And there are many days, weeks and even months where I don't even think of them. But then there are days like today where something hits and it hits hard." She sighed. "It's interesting, isn't it, how the smallest things can open the gates. Like seeing how nice someone treats their employees."

He reached out, slowly, then laid a hand on top of hers. This time the heat that spread was one of comfort, of support and understanding.

Silence descended. She was, she realized, not uncomfortable as they sat there. No, she was feeling… heard. Respected.

"I was told," he said quietly, "grief comes in waves.

It starts off like a tsunami, and you think there's no possible way you can get out from under it. Then the waves get a little more manageable. Over time, they become ripples. But you'll still occasionally have that moment, that memory, that thought that knocks you off your feet. And that's okay."

She tilted her head. "I like that." She laid her fingers on top of his, the sight of their hands atop one another comforting. "I also heard that sometimes we hang on to grief because we're too frightened of who we are without it."

He stared at her, his face unreadable. She kept her hand on his, grateful when he didn't pull away. Had she gone too far? She saw so much of herself in Damon, the holding back to keep himself safe. But perhaps, after she had trusted him, he might feel the same way.

This time the silence that followed carried an edge. Damon held her gaze for what felt like forever before he gave her a small, opaque smile that made her feel cold. "Perhaps."

He squeezed her hand, stood and retreated back to his desk.

Dismissed, quickly and effectively. She might have been ready to unburden some of her darkest moments, to share with the man who was to become her lover. Clearly, he wasn't.

No reason for him to share, she reminded herself as she quietly excused herself and walked back to her office. *You're not his girlfriend.*

She knew a little about his past. A framed obituary in the lobby included a brief mention that a drunk driver had killed David and Helen Bradford when Damon had been in his senior year of college. Evolet hadn't been able to bring herself to do an online search to learn more. It had felt too much like an invasion of privacy if Damon didn't want to talk about it.

She closed the door to her office and sank down into her chair. She picked up a pencil, twirled it absently in her fingers, set it back down. She'd taken a small risk, and while the moment of connection over loss had been affirming, Damon's lack of reciprocity had been a much-needed reminder as to what their arrangement was—as well as what it would never be.

Although perhaps after what had just happened, Damon would want to terminate their agreement. Just the thought twisted her stomach into knots.

Taking a deep breath, she focused on her computer and began to respond to the emails that had piled up in her inbox. Her fingers itched for her bow, to play a song or two and settle the somber restlessness inside her.

Later, she promised herself. Later she would play. And whatever came after that, she would deal with it.

Even if she dealt with it alone.

CHAPTER ELEVEN

DAMON KNOCKED ON the door to Evolet's office. At her soft "Enter," he twisted the knob and stepped inside, closing the door behind him.

She looked up from her computer, a small smile crossing her face. Relief filtered through him. He knew he'd been borderline rude with his response to her gentle prompt on his own sorrow. It hadn't been fair to prod her to share when he had no intention of doing so.

Although it went much deeper than simply not wanting to open up. Digging down into the depths of his grief, of ripping open a wound that had taken so long to repair to the point he could function was too much. Even just recalling memories of his parents sent pain lancing through him. While he appreciated the intention behind the hanging of the obituary in the lobby, an action taken in the weeks after his parents' deaths when there had been an interim CEO, he avoided looking at it every time he walked through.

"Is everything okay?"

He refocused on Evolet, who was watching him with guarded cautiousness. God, he felt like a cad. She'd trusted him with something incredibly precious—not just once with asking him to be her lover, but twice by sharing such an intimate part of her history.

"I don't talk about my parents."

She turned then to face him completely, folding her hands on the desk and fixing him with that golden gaze.

"I won't ever ask you to. I know what arrangement we have, Damon, and I—"

"You misunderstand," he said, trying to suppress the frustration in his voice. "It's cliché to say that it's not you, it's me, but it's true. Talking about them…" He paused, hardened his heart against the past straining to break free. "It hurts too much. I fell into a very dark place after they passed."

Memories of waking up, vivid nightmares of his parents' accident giving way to the crushing reality that they were gone, flashed through him. He had loved his parents, and they had loved him. But that love had come with a heavy price in the wake of loss.

A price he would never pay again.

Her face softened. "You must have loved them very much."

"I still do."

She stood and came around the desk. Before he could move, she took his hand just as he had taken hers in his office. Her fingers were so much smaller than his, pale and elegant against his skin.

"I understand."

Just like that, he was forgiven. Humbled, unsettled by her simple acceptance, he nodded at her computer. "Any word?"

The tension in the room bled out as she circled back around her desk and blew out a frustrated breath.

"No." She glanced at him, then laughed. "You've been checking, too, haven't you?"

He grinned. "I feel like a little kid at Christmas waiting for his present to arrive." He glanced down at his watch, then groaned. "And it's only ten o'clock."

Evolet sighed. "How am I going to survive the weekend?"

As soon as the words were out of her mouth, her head jerked up as her eyes darkened. His mind scrambled, thoughts of business scattering as possibilities opened before him, each idea more sensual and tantalizing until he was so hard it was almost painful.

The proposal had been submitted. Evolet would move to a different department on Monday. Nothing was stopping him now from fulfilling her request.

"Let's go."

Her eyes widened. "Go?"

"It's Friday." He walked closer until he was just on the other side of her desk. "The proposal is submitted. Bengtsson will take at least a week, possibly two, to review the proposals. On the off chance he jumps the gun, I have my phone on me."

"But you're the CEO. What if something comes up?"

"I told Julie I would be available off-site by phone. I also told her I was giving you the rest of the day off to thank you for your hard work."

She worried her lower lip with her teeth. "And our… arrangement… I know you didn't want me to be working for you…"

"As of Monday, you'll be reporting to my chief engineer, Nathaniel Pratt, and serving in a temporary role as executive assistant to three of his engineers. I've wanted to try out the concept of having assistants for our engineers for some time, and testing it out through the remainder of your contract is the perfect opportunity."

"Don't you still need an assistant?"

"Louise requested an extension of her maternity leave. She'll be gone for up to a year. One of the secretaries who works under Julie has been jumping at the chance to become an executive assistant, and this will give him a chance to get some experience." He arched an eyebrow. "Any other roadblocks you'd like to throw in my way?"

When she didn't answer, he held out his hand, his lips tilting up into a smile that challenged her to take a risk. "Let's play hooky, Evolet."

She stared at the outstretched hand. He heard the sharp inhale of her breath, watched as her breasts rose and fell beneath the silky white material of her shirt.

Unease skittered through him. Had she changed her mind?

Then she reached out, took his hand and gave him a smile that slipped past his desire and stirred something deep inside him. "Okay."

Fifteen minutes later they were pulling out of the parking garage, Damon behind the wheel of a vintage silver Aston Martin and Evolet's cello secured in the trunk.

"Did you have dreams of being a spy as a boy?" Evolet asked teasingly as he pulled out into the glorious mess of New York City traffic.

"What do you mean 'did'?"

He savored the burst of laughter, the uninhibited smile that made Evolet's eyes crinkle. The light turned green, and a cacophony of car horns blared behind them. As much as he appreciated having his own time, indulging in the seclusion of his office or traveling upstate to his family's estate in the Catskills, he took great joy in the city that had embraced his grandfather's company decades ago.

The simple pleasure of the moment, of leaving work early, had him letting down his guard. His fingers curled around the steering wheel as the car surged forward. The sensation of cool, smooth leather beneath his hands stirred a memory—the first time his father had let him drive the Aston Martin, punching up the volume of his favorite spy movie's iconic theme music.

"The car belonged to my father."

The words came out before he could stop them. He waited for the stab of pain, the curtain of depression to descend and blight out the brightness of the day.

Yet it didn't come. The sadness was there, yes. But mostly he just felt the nostalgic warmth of one of the happiest times in his life.

"He had very good taste."

The simple reply, one that accepted the tiny bit he'd shared and didn't pry for more, helped him relax once more. Whether Evolet understood the significance of the simple admission or not, it felt surprisingly good to share something about his father. He hoped, too, it made up in some small part for his boorishness earlier.

"Where to?"

He felt her glance, sensed her confusion. Had she imagined he would just whisk her away to a hotel, have his way with her and then disappear?

No. He wanted nothing more than to slip that proper blouse off her shoulders, slide the skirt from her waist and finally make his most erotic fantasies come to life. But Evolet deserved more than just sex. If the woman wasn't working or practicing in the park, she was playing with the symphony or spending time with her adoptive mother.

She deserved a day without schedules, tasks and rushing to get to the next thing on her to-do list. She deserved a day just about her.

"Um…"

He reached over and grabbed her hand. She started, her body tensing a moment before she relaxed. When she twined her fingers through his, he felt the satisfaction of her acquiescence all the way to his bones.

"Where's somewhere in New York you've always wanted to go but never have?"

At the next stoplight he glanced over to see another smile spreading across her face, this one shy and sweet.

"The Empire State Building."

He guided the car down FDR Drive, the city gleaming under the morning sunlight to their left and the river shimmering to their right. They rode the elevator to the top of the Empire State Building.

When they walked out onto the observation deck, the sheer joy on Evolet's face made his chest fill with a happiness he hadn't experienced in a very long time. They slipped quarters into the coin-operated binoculars and circled the deck at least four times.

"That was incredible," Evolet gushed as they walked back out onto Thirty-Fourth Street and toward the private parking garage Damon had booked. "I can't wait to tell Constanza."

"Where does she live?"

Damon inwardly swore as Evolet's face dimmed.

"A memory care facility across the river. It's one of the best in the tristate area."

He frowned. "That sounds expensive."

Evolet shrugged. "Constanza's son, Samuel, is ten years older than me. He works as a welder and pays for over half. I contribute what I can."

His esteem for Evolet had already been high. Now, as she walked alongside him, her face tilted up to the sun, it skyrocketed. There were so many layers to this fascinating woman, each one more intriguing than the last.

He whisked her to a quiet French bistro off Union Square for a late lunch, where they dined on mushroom ravioli smothered in truffle fondue sauce and pan-seared salmon. They shared a dessert of poached pear topped with vanilla ice cream. After he grudgingly let her pay for the tip, he drove her to the Morgan Library and Museum, taking joy out of watching her mouth drop open at the sight of the three stories of walnut bookcases packed with manuscripts and the intricately painted arched ceiling.

As the sun slid across the sky, he drove back toward Billionaires' Row. The glass exterior of the One57 building that housed a hotel and condominiums, including Damon's own penthouse, glinted in the pinkening light of twilight.

"I'd like to take you one more place."

Evolet chuckled softly. Her eyes were closed, her lashes dark against her skin. "Just one more? I feel like I've lived more in one day than I have my entire life."

Her innocent words wrapped around him. When he'd taken Natalie out to dinner, the final bill had been more than what he'd spent so far today. Never had Natalie reacted with such unbridled excitement or joy. Nor had he enjoyed himself half as much.

"Come to my penthouse."

Her eyes shot open. He pulled the car off to the side of the road and turned so he was facing her.

"Your penthouse," Evolet echoed quietly.

"Yes." He gave in to the temptation that had been haunting him all day and reached out, cupping her face in his palm.

All around them, New York continued its frantic pace. Taxis and motorcycles battled for space with horns honking and tires screeching. A sidewalk musician wailed out a jazzy tune on a saxophone. Pedestrians streamed by, laughing, conversing and shouting as night descended.

But inside the car, only Evolet existed. Evolet and this moment.

"I'd like that."

Desire welled inside him, propelled him forward as he pulled her closer. Her lips parted, and their mouths met in a kiss that swept through him like wildfire.

As he pulled back into traffic and guided his car toward Billionaires' Row, he focused on the anticipation, the hot pulse of hunger.

And ignored the emotions whispering beneath the currents of his need.

CHAPTER TWELVE

EVOLET TURNED IN a circle, trying and failing to keep her mouth from dropping open. Three of the walls of Damon's living room were tinted glass with the kind of views of Midtown and Central Park some people would kill for. The room still had the old-library feel the Bradford Global office did. But here there was a touch of modern—soft gray leather furniture, black lamps and moody photographs of what she guessed was the Hudson River Valley upstate. On the other side of the glass, just off the kitchen that sported granite countertops and soft golden lighting underneath the custom black cabinets, was a balcony with artfully arranged plants and cozy outdoor furniture. If she craned her head enough, she could spot the pool at the far end.

"Pinch me."

"What?"

"This has to be a dream," she said breathlessly. "I can't believe real people live like this." She shot him a bashful smile over her shoulder before looking out over the park again. "Sorry. I live in a two-bedroom three-story walk-up in East Harlem. This is just...unreal."

Damon came up behind her, so close she could feel the heat from his body. "I'm glad you like it."

His voice seeped into her veins. She took a risk and leaned back, sighing as her back rested against his muscular chest. Slowly, his arms twined about her waist, then turned her to face him before he lowered his lips to hers.

The kiss was no less powerful than the ones they'd already shared. But it was different, gentler, testing, even as his hands spread possessively across her back.

Nerves skittered across her skin. What if she disappointed him? What if they'd built up this attraction into something far more passionate than what the actual event would bring?

Sensing her sudden hesitancy, Damon pulled back but kept her tight in the circle of his arms.

"I want you, Evolet," he grated out. "But I won't take anything you're not ready to give. It's your choice." His breath rushed out. "It's always your choice."

That he would hold himself back, offer her a choice even as she saw the pulse pounding at the base of his throat, felt the restrained passion in hands that cradled hers like she was made of glass dissolved her resistance as if it had never existed.

"I'm ready."

Damon moved as soon as the words were uttered. He picked her up in his arms and carried her into his bedroom. She got a quick impression of dark navy walls and a massive bed before he set her on her feet. He reached over, flicked on a lamp and then moved his hands over her. Her blouse disappeared over her head, her bra unclipped in a matter of seconds.

"You've done that before," she said, amused.

"I have." His eyes feasted on her bare breasts. "But this…"

One hand came up, cupped the fullness of her breast. She moaned as his thumb whispered across her nipple.

"Evolet, you are so beautiful."

With that pronouncement lingering seductively in the air, he leaned down and captured her nipple in his mouth. Each flick of his tongue, each gentle suck sent her spiraling higher. He lavished the same attention on her other breast, driving her to distraction so that she didn't even register his fingers unbuttoning her skirt or sliding the material down until cool air kissed her naked legs.

Damon looked down, swore.

"What?" She glanced down, shyness threatening to overtake her as she realized she'd worn simple nude-colored panties instead of the red lacy lingerie she'd purchased after Damon had accepted her deal.

"Did I say beautiful?" He sank to his knees, captured her hips in an iron grip that made her knees weak. "Gorgeous." He kissed the sensitive skin above the fabric "Exquisite." Another kiss to her core, now throbbing with need. "Stunning."

He skimmed up her body so quickly she didn't have time to catch her breath. He scooped her up into his arms once more, then laid her on the bed as he raked her with a hungry gaze.

"Much as I like the panties," he said, his voice husky as he hooked his fingers into the material, "I want to see you naked."

And she wanted him to see her naked. Charged with confidence and desire, she lifted her hips, savored the parting of his lips and the lascivious gleam in his eyes.

Then she was bare. Shyness teased her, but she stayed still, watching him watch her. Each passing second increased the ache until she was filled with it, a pressure building in her chest as her body demanded satisfaction.

Finally, he moved, stripping off his clothes with decisive movements, tossing his dress shirt, pants and belt onto the floor. Was it odd to describe a man as beautiful? *Handsome* didn't do justice to his body, hard ridges and lean muscles honed by time and discipline. His erection jutted out proudly.

He sat on the edge of the bed and skimmed a finger over her skin. The touch was featherlight, but the trail of heat he left behind sank into her, made her bow off the bed as he drew patterns on her belly, her thighs.

Her legs bent, shifting restlessly.

"Damon...please..."

He moved over. His body settled on top of hers, a solid comforting weight that pressed her deeper into the embrace of the bed. The thrill of having his naked skin against hers nearly made her come undone as he kissed her again, slowly, romantically. As the golden light of the lamp caressed the angles and planes of his body, he made his way down hers with kisses, soft nips and gentle caresses that heated her blood and made her flush with need. When he placed his mouth on her most sensitive skin, she felt that blessed pleasure growing inside her, climbing higher and higher...

He stopped. She started to sit up, to protest, but he moved quickly, capturing her hands in his as he claimed her lips.

"I want to be inside you this first time." He kissed her cheek, the curve of her jaw, pressed the sweetest of kisses to her shoulder. "I want to feel you shatter around me."

Her thighs parted to cradle his weight. He groaned as her wet heat pressed against his hard length, and she smiled with sheer feminine satisfaction that she could bring this man just as close to the edge as he brought her.

"One moment," he ground out.

He rolled off of her and pulled a condom from the nightstand drawer. She watched as he rolled it onto his erection, her breath coming out in short pants as his fingers glided up and down. She reached for him, wanting to touch, but he caught her wrist and pinned it above her head as he lowered himself back down to her.

"I'm not going to have your first time involve me embarrassing myself."

"Do I drive you that wild?" she asked with a smile, her other hand skating down his back and slipping between their bodies to graze his him. He hissed, grabbed her questing hand and pinned it next to her head.

"Minx."

Her smile faded as she stared deep into his eyes.

"Damon…"

He watched her.

"Make love to me."

He released her hands and wrapped her in a strong embrace as he pressed against her. Her body welcomed him, pulled him deeper. There was a moment of pain, and she couldn't hold back her slight cry. He paused, soothed, kissed her eyelids, the tip of her nose as he held her tighter and whispered sweet nothings in her ear.

Slowly, her body relaxed, accepted him. He began to move with languid strokes that restoked the flames of desire. She rocked against him in an instinctive rhythm.

Sighs turned to gasps. Dampness slicked their skin as they climbed higher, their bodies racing to the top. He braced himself on his elbows, lifted just enough to watch her face.

"Damon… Damon, I can't…"

"Let go. Let go for me, Evolet."

She let herself fly over the edge, felt sensation splinter then fracture into thousands of dazzling bursts of pleasure. She cried out again, this time in ecstasy, her legs coming up and wrapping around his waist as she pulled him to her.

He whispered her name, followed her a moment later. He shuddered, his arms clamped around her like a vice.

Slowly, so slowly, they drifted down, heartbeats slowing, breaths quieting as they lay tangled up in each other. Evolet's fingers drifted up and down his back—her lover's back—and she sighed in pleasured satisfaction. Damon brushed a soft kiss to her cheek.

Never had she felt so aware of her body, so sure of herself, so reckless in giving rather than protecting.

Reality tried to intrude, to remind her that he was her lover for just tonight, that to lie with him like this in the aftermath of their lovemaking was almost more of an intimacy than what they had just shared.

But she would not deny herself. Days, months, years later, when she looked back on her first time, she would relive the seduction, the foreplay, the incredible act of joining her body with his.

With the remnants of physical pleasure still flickering inside her, a pleasure made all the more potent by embracing the emotions she'd fought so hard to keep at bay, she closed her eyes and drifted off to sleep.

* * *

Damon looked up as Evolet padded into the kitchen, her hair rumpled and her eyes sleepy. The sight of her in one of his T-shirts with those beautiful legs bare sent a bolt of possessiveness through him.

Had it really been two days since he'd first taken her to bed? He hadn't planned on inviting her to stay the whole weekend. That first night they'd awoken in each other's arms around midnight. When she'd turned to him with a smile and a whispered thank-you, he'd suddenly wanted to extend the night just a little longer. He'd carried her into the bathroom, drawn a hot bath and cradled her in his arms as he'd washed away the remnants of her first time. His own tenderness had surprised him. He hadn't been prepared for how intense their first time together would be, the knowledge that not only had he been her first lover but her first choice, her only choice. It had humbled him, touched a part of him he hadn't known existed and made him want to gather her in his arms and care for her.

And then she'd turned to him, rising up like a siren with water sluicing down over her skin, beading on the tips of her breasts, as she'd arched her body and rubbed herself against him before taking him in hand and stroking him to the point of madness. He'd barely remembered to extract himself long enough to grab a condom out of the nightstand before sinking inside her once more.

Previous affairs had been mutually enjoyed, pleasant, sexy, even invigorating. But never had a woman slipped past his defenses and stirred more than the faintest feelings of companionship.

They'd woken Saturday morning, ordered breakfast

and eaten in bed. He'd had a swimming suit delivered so she could enjoy the heated pool he so rarely used. Although, he admitted to himself, it hadn't been just for her. Watching her body glide through the water had made him so hard he'd whisked her back inside and made love to her on the couch. Afternoon had turned into evening, and when she'd fallen asleep on him while they were watching a movie, he'd carried her back to his bed.

He'd never enjoyed time with a woman so much as he had enjoyed the past couple of days. And that put him on guard. This arrangement was supposed to be about a mutually pleasurable affair, introducing a woman he found interesting and intriguing to sex, not playing house.

Remember that, he ordered himself as he took a sip of coffee and inwardly swore as the scalding liquid burned his tongue.

"Good morning." He kept his tone casual, stayed with the barrier of the countertop between them.

Her smile punched him in the gut, sleepy and with a hint of bashfulness as she circled around the kitchen island, raised up on her toes and grazed his stubbled cheek with a kiss. "Good morning."

The husky thread in her voice had his muscles tightening. He forced the desire back and returned her smile.

"Did you sleep well?"

"Aside from getting woken up around midnight, yes," she teased as she checked him with her hip on the way to the coffee machine.

They'd turned to each other in the night, waking to find themselves wrapped around each other. He hadn't been gentle, but then neither had she. They'd devoured each other, bodies molded together as they caressed, demanded, took everything they could give each other.

It still wasn't enough, he thought as his eyes drifted down over her rear, her thighs, her bare feet.

Would it ever be enough?

The thought had him turning away from the intoxicating sight of her and back to the stove.

"I made breakfast. Eggs, bacon and pancakes if you're hungry."

As he flipped the last pancake, her arms wound around his waist. He tensed before forcing himself to relax. His own musings and hang-ups could take a break for just a little longer.

"Thank you," she whispered as she rested her cheek against his back.

He laid the spatula down and turned, wrapped his arms gently around her and breathed in the scent of her. "For?"

She gestured to the stove, her eyes suspiciously bright. "For breakfast. For...all of it."

She started to pull away, but he held tighter.

"What is it?"

Her throat worked as she swallowed hard, her gaze fixed on the plates of food.

"The last time someone made me breakfast was Constanza." Her small smile didn't reach her eyes. "That was the first thing she did that got through to me. It's not like I went hungry in my other foster homes," she added quickly, "but breakfast was usually Pop-Tarts, pre-made waffles, that kind of thing. But Constanza..." Her smile grew, her eyes crinkling at the corners as happiness chased away some of the sorrow.

"My first morning I came down and she had made me Haitian patties and *mais moulin ak zepina*—pastries stuffed with spicy beef and cornmeal grits with spinach. It was one of the most delicious meals I'd ever eaten." She looked up at him then, and the mix of sadness with the beauty of nostalgia made his heart hammer in his chest.

"She looked at me and smoothed my hair back from my face and said, 'I made you breakfast, Evie.' And it was so simple, but she'd done it for me, just for me, and she remembered my name."

She suddenly shook her head and tried once more to pull away. His arms tightened around her.

"Sorry." She brushed the heel of her hand against her cheek to wipe away a wayward tear. "I guess sex and breakfast make me emotional."

"Don't do that."

Her head snapped up. "Do what?"

"Don't make excuses for how you feel." He captured her chin in his grip so she couldn't look away. "I can hear in your voice how much she means to you. Don't run from what you had with her—or what you still have even though it looks different than it used to."

"Thank you." She glanced down at her feet.

"What?"

"Just…" She sucked in a breath and then looked back up. "Doesn't that apply to you, too?"

He froze.

"Sorry—"

"You still have Constanza," he broke in. "You have someone. I don't."

She watched him for another long moment. Then,

as if sensing she'd pushed enough, she simply said "Okay" and started to pull away.

Conscious of the tension that had descended between them, he tugged her back and dropped a light kiss on her forehead. "Let's eat on the balcony."

Minutes later, between the food and the warmth of the morning sun, the mood had shifted back to relaxed.

"I'll probably head home after breakfast."

She said it nonchalantly, not meeting his gaze as she speared a piece of egg with her fork.

He nodded even as his chest tightened. "I can drive you."

"No, thanks." She smiled slightly. "I like the subway."

"You *like* the subway?"

"Mmm-hmm. I'm sure part of it is finding my love of music in the tunnels, that nostalgia that pulls me back. But part of it..."

Her voice trailed off as she frowned. Before he could question himself, he rose and sat in one of the chairs across from her.

"Part of it?" he prompted.

The grin she shot him warmed his body. "You make it hard to keep myself all locked up when you're such a darn good listener."

"I like listening to you talk."

And he did. He liked her bravado, her honesty, her spunky fire.

"I'm really good at holding myself back. A skill you pick up pretty quickly when you get bounced from home to home. But on the subway..." She smiled. "Everyone's doing their own thing, but they also show all these pieces of themselves, little vignettes of their lives. It makes me feel connected."

"Do you want to feel connected?"

The frown returned. "I didn't used to." She shrugged. "Maybe I'm just getting older."

This time he laughed. "How old are you again?"

"Twenty-five."

He groaned. "God save me from women in their twenties who think they're old."

When she laughed again, tossing her head back with carefree abandon, the sound rippling across his skin, he took a chance and leaped.

"What would you think about extending our arrangement?"

She fell silent almost immediately, her eyes widening. "What?"

"I'd like to see you again."

"As in…?"

"Not a relationship per se. That's not what either of us is looking for. But I'd like to see you again, spend time with you…" His eyes drifted down to her legs, and he shot her a wicked smile. "Both in and out of bed."

She swallowed hard. "For how long?"

He paused. The part of him that was enjoying her didn't want to say. But it would be in both their interests to put an end date to whatever relationship they carried on. Something that kept things fun and light.

"Through the duration of your contract with Bradford Global." Just a little over a month. Enough to enjoy, but not long enough to get attached.

The seconds dragged out. Then, at last, she smiled.

"I'd like that."

Relief swept through him. It shouldn't have mattered, but it did.

"Good. Did you have anything on your schedule for today?"

"I need to practice later, but that's it."

"Perfect."

He plucked the fork from her fingers, picked her up around the waist and threw her over his shoulder, carrying her inside as she laughingly protested. The protests died on her lips as he laid her down on his bed, pulled the shirt over her head and lost himself in the pleasures of her body.

CHAPTER THIRTEEN

DAMON STARED AT his computer. He'd read the latest report from the manufacturing plant in Texas at least three times, and he still had no idea what was in it. In the last two weeks, his legendary focus had slipped. He still showed up to work early, accomplished his tasks, oversaw meetings and swiftly put out fires, from budgeting issues to a disagreement between two of his engineers.

But in the back of his mind, always, was Evolet.

It had been two weeks since she'd spent the weekend with him. During the day, they maintained a professional rapport. No stolen kisses, no frantic embraces behind closed doors. He was already straining his personal sense of ethics by indulging in an affair with someone on the Bradford Global payroll. Evolet understood. That she did, and respected his stance, just made him like her more.

And that was a problem. He didn't want to like her. He didn't want to reach for her when he woke up or think about her on the nights she spent at her apartment.

He was getting in too deep. Too deep, but he couldn't

bring himself to end it. Not when they had such a short amount of time left.

Four more weeks. Four more weeks, and then she would move on. Their affair would end, and he could return to the life he'd led before she'd walked into his life.

The thought should have relieved him. Instead, it just made him feel depressed.

His phone vibrated, pulling his attention back from his morbid musings. He glanced at the email alert and then smiled as satisfaction returned him to the present. He walked down the hall at a brisk clip.

"There's an update from Royal Air," he said as he walked into Evolet's office.

She sat up straight, alert and ready. "And?"

"Bengtsson has selected two to move forward. Including," he said as pride filled his chest, "Bradford Global."

A smile broke across her face. She clapped her hands as a delighted laugh escaped her lips. "That's incredible!"

"Yes, but there's a catch. The CEO, Bryant Bengtsson, wants representatives from the final two to meet with him. A final interview of sorts before he makes his decision. He's invited two from each company." Damon looked up at her. "I want you to go with me."

Her eyes widened. "Me?"

"You know that proposal as well as I do, perhaps even better."

"And you want me to go with you to Sweden?"

"Not Sweden," he said with a smile. "We're flying to Bali."

* * *

Evolet looked down at the cobalt-blue waters of the
Pacific. She'd never been to the West Coast, and now
she was flying across it in a private jet.

She stole a glance at Damon. They'd both read and
reread the proposal, privately and out loud. They'd
talked through potential questions Bengtsson might
throw at them, discussed risks and benefits.

Finally, she'd needed a break and had moved to the
leather sofa that stretched along one wall of the plane.

Not just a break from work, but also from the tur
moil still churning inside her.

The past two weeks with Damon had been some of
the best of her life. More often than not, she spent the
night at his penthouse, making love in his bed, the jet
tub, the thick rug in front of the fireplace. She cooked
him meals, replicating some of the Haitian dishes Constanza had taught her. They talked about music, books,
movies, debated over which art pieces they'd liked best
when they'd visited the Met and the places they wanted
to travel. The more time they spent together, the more
she shared about her upbringing with Constanza, her
late-in-life musical training.

They talked about everything but Damon.

A soft sigh escaped her. It was his prerogative to
keep his own secrets. He was a considerate, generous
lover, thoughtful of her, yet still he held back. When
she shared her own stories, like the first time she'd seen
the Central Park Carousel, he'd held her in the circle
of his arms, kissed her forehead and murmured quiet
words that had wrapped around her in a comforting
embrace. She hadn't anticipated letting herself become

so vulnerable. She hadn't opened up to anyone except for Constanza in years. Yet it had happened naturally, her barriers coming down as she shared her body, and then the deepest parts of herself, with a man who listened, who cared and encouraged her.

And yet still he remained silent on his own past, his own desires beyond what he wanted for Bradford Global.

The more time she spent with him, the more vulnerable she allowed herself to be, the more acutely she felt his lack of confidence in her. In four weeks, she would be gone, both from Bradford Global and from Damon Bradford's life.

The longer she indulged in this affair, the harder it became to contemplate walking away.

Stop it, she ordered herself as she rubbed at her temple. He'd set boundaries, clear ones. If they were in an actual relationship, that would have been one thing, but they weren't. They were casual lovers.

She let her head drop back against the arm of the couch. The hum of the engine and the events of the past day made her eyelids heavy.

"There's a bedroom in the back of the plane."

She opened her eyes to see Damon crouched next to her. He reached out and smoothed a strand of hair back from her face, the simple gesture making her breath catch in her throat.

"That sounds nice."

He held out his hand and pulled her to her feet. "I'll walk you back."

She shook her head as she walked into the small room. A queen-sized bed covered in a silky emerald comforter took up most of the space, with a bathroom at the back and a closet off to the side. "This is amazing."

"I'm glad you like it." Damon paused. "Sit with me a moment."

Suddenly on guard, Evolet sat down with him on the edge of the bed. He didn't reach for her, didn't touch her, just speared her with a gaze that was simultaneously distant and wary.

"I told you before I don't talk about my parents. That it's too painful." At Evolet's nod, he continued. "What happened to them changed my life. The world I knew was gone in an instant. It showed me that things like love and happiness can be taken without warning. It's why I focused on Bradford Global. There are risks, but there's also control."

Evolet's fingers dug into the bedspread. She wanted to reach out, to smooth her hand over Damon's face and offer him comfort. But she wasn't sure where this confession was headed, what he needed from her.

"Continuing my family's legacy has given me purpose. It's filled my life."

But has it?

It was eerie to hear him say the same words she herself would have said just weeks ago, to notice the intensity running through his voice, as if he were trying to convince himself that what he said was truth.

"I'm glad you found something," she said carefully.

"Thank you." He breathed in. "I'm sharing this with you because I know we've become close the last couple of weeks. I want to continue our arrangement. But," he added gently, "I wanted to reiterate that anything beyond these weeks isn't an option. A relationship, love, none of that is in my future."

She willed herself not to cry. He was only repeating what she'd already known. But God, it hurt so much more after the past couple of weeks together.

"I understand." She said the words carefully, taking care to enunciate each one and keep her tone neutral. "Have I given you any reason to think I might ask or demand more after this is over?"

He blinked. "No."

"Okay." She reached over and laid a gentle hand on top of his. "I've been enjoying our time together, Damon."

He stared down at her hand.

"I have, too." He let out a quiet, derisive chuckle. "I like you. I don't want to hurt you or make you think that something more could happen. I'm not capable of it."

Evolet's heart cracked for the man before her, a man she had come to care very deeply for in such a short amount of time. She knew what it felt like that, to withdraw so deeply into oneself to keep pain at bay. But she had missed out on so much. She'd lived more in the past month than she had her entire life. She wanted that for Damon, too, this man who listened and cared and worked so hard.

Except he wasn't ready. She wouldn't push him, wouldn't cause him pain when he had reestablished the boundary between them.

So she offered him comfort the only way he would accept. She leaned forward, pressed a kiss to his cheek. He turned his head and captured her lips with his. The kiss catapulted from slow and tender into a desperate craving. With a groan he spun, pressing her down onto the bed. He yanked her shirt over her head, captured a nipple in his mouth as she arched over his arm.

He suddenly stopped as he cursed.

"What?" she asked breathlessly.

"Condom."

She paused. "I…um, I started the pill after you accepted my proposal. I didn't say anything because I figured you would want the extra protection and I was nervous about bringing it up—"

He cut off her words by wrapping one hand around her neck and hauling her against him for another kiss.

"You just might kill me yet," he growled against her mouth.

Their clothes ended up in a pile on the floor. He grabbed her hips and drove inside her.

She closed around him as if he'd been made for her. His head dropped to her shoulder. He slid out, then back in.

"God, Evolet." He moved inside her, each thrust driving her higher.

"Faster," she urged him in a throaty whisper.

"No." He lifted his head and smiled down at her. "I've never made love bare, and I intend to savor every moment."

His words hit her, the intimacy of what they were sharing made all the more potent by his admission. It made her wonder, made her hope that perhaps, with time, he might let his guard down even more.

He sank deeper inside her, moving with languid strokes of his hips, pressing his body fully against hers. His hands moved over her with a sensual mastery that stole her breath. The heat that seemed to always burn between them rose up and consumed them both as she cried out and he poured himself into her.

CHAPTER FOURTEEN

A THIN, hazy mist hung over the jungle's rich green foliage. The blue waters of the Bali Sea sparkled beneath the sun as waves pounded the beach below.

Evolet leaned against the balcony railing and sighed in pleasure. It was hard to believe that just a day ago she had been surrounded by concrete and steel, and now there was nothing but wilderness and ocean as far as she could see.

Perched on top of a cliff that sloped down to a private beach, the Bali Regency Resort combined elegance with the kind of relaxation one could only find at an exotic getaway. Stone villas were scattered among the trees, connected by weaving stone paths and drives. Pergolas beckoned guests to rest beneath shady trees, while wooden signs directed visitors to the spa, the oceanside restaurant and the departure points for tours of nearby temples and even a volcano. Their villa, a two-bedroom mini mansion situated on top of an ocean cliff, boasted a private pool among tall grasses and giant fuchsia-colored blooms, a private infinity pool outside the bedroom Damon had gestured for her to take and even a private cinema. It had been during her quick snooping through the villa that she'd discovered this balcony off of an upstairs library.

She heard the door behind her creak softly.

"This is incredible."

He came up behind her, hands settling on her waist. She stiffened for the briefest of moments, then forced herself to relax and lean back against his chest. If she closed her eyes for a moment, she could almost imagine they were here for pleasure instead of just business.

"I'm glad you're enjoying it."

"I am. But," she added as she turned in the circle of his arms, "we have work to do."

He leaned down, brushed his lips across her neck. "Yes."

"Damon…" She put her hands on his chest, intending to push him away. When he kissed her neck, her fingers relaxed against the softness of his shirt. "What are you doing?"

"I'm restless." He straightened, a frown crossing his face. "I've never been restless before a meeting with a client."

"And taunting me helps you relax?"

A wicked smile flashed. "No. But it does help me think of other things."

He kissed her, the simple caress quickly turning heated as his tongue teased the seam of her lips and then slipped into her mouth. She returned every touch, savored the taste of him as her fingers wound in his hair.

"All right," he said as he pulled back. She was satisfied to hear his breathing was just as ragged as hers.

"We've been asked to attend a dinner with Bengtsson, his wife and the other company at eight."

Panic suddenly seized her. "What kind of dinner?"

"The kind where you eat."

She smacked him on the shoulder. "Like fancy? I didn't bring any clothes like that, just a couple work outfits and some casual wear. I thought we'd be dealing with Bengtsson in a conference room."

He gently cupped her elbows and tugged her closer. "Is this important to you?"

"It is. I want to represent Bradford Global well. That means looking the part, too."

This time his smile warmed her in an entirely different way.

"That's why I brought you with me."

"To wear fancy clothes?"

He laughed. "No. Because you care. And because you know that bid inside and out. Bengtsson is a good man, but he's crafty. He doesn't pull punches, and he enjoys trying to trip people up."

"Not giving me a lot of reason to feel confident here."

He squeezed her arms in a gesture of affection that unsettled her more than his kiss had. "Be yourself, Evolet. Be yourself and show Bengtsson an ounce of the knowledge and passion you have for this project, and I know we'll get it."

She blinked as the floor dropped out from under her. She knew how much the company meant to him. That he trusted her to this degree with what she had heard multiple people talking about as the biggest project Bradford Global had ever gone after thrilled and terrified her.

"Okay. No pressure. Where does one find clothes around here that would help me go up against a crafty CEO?"

Ten minutes later Evolet browsed through a boutique on the lower level of the resort's main building. Every now and then she glanced away from the jaw-dropping price tags and out at the sea. She saw the ocean on a regular basis living on the East Coast. But seeing it here, surrounded by so much natural beauty, was a different experience entirely.

She had just about given up when she spied a flash of green in the back corner. She grabbed the hanger and pulled the dress out, a smile spreading across her face.

It was perfect. Elegant, tasteful, with a hint of sexiness that would make her feel like she belonged among the elite guests at tonight's dinner.

And hopefully, she thought with a small smile, it would knock Damon's socks off.

Damon leaned against the stone wall that bordered the private terrace Bengtsson had booked for tonight's dinner and sipped a glass of champagne. Jazz played quietly from speakers hidden among the foliage. Crowley's chief operations and finance officers had been sent in the CEO's stead. While Damon believed in showing his personal investment in his clients and their contracts, Crowley was still a worthy opponent. Both of the executives were respected in the manufacturing community and very good at their jobs.

He took another sip of champagne and glanced toward the stone steps. Evolet had come back from her shopping with a bag in hand and a feminine smile on her face that had teased him. She'd told him to go on without her, promising that she would arrive before the dinner started.

Guilt whispered through him. Talking with her on the plane and reminding her that their affair could go no further than it already had had seemed like the logical thing to do. Every now and then he would catch Evolet looking at him, an emotion flickering in her eyes that both thrilled and terrified him. He suspected she was coming to feel more for him than what he could give in return.

Except she hadn't reacted the way he'd anticipated. There had been a flash of hurt, yes. But then she had handled it decorously, making him wonder if the hurt had been more because he'd brought it up when she hadn't done anything overt to make him doubt her.

That she had handled it so well had done the opposite of reassuring him. No, her sedate response had slipped under his skin, an uncomfortable sensation that prickled and taunted. He had tried to dissect it. But then he'd seen her standing at the balcony looking out over the ocean, blond hair streaming down her back, and cursed himself. He was getting exactly what he wanted. He was in Bali with a woman he found captivating, a woman whose company he enjoyed both in and out of bed.

He needed to accept that things were fine just the way they were and focus his attention on the matter at hand: securing the Royal Air contract.

"Ah, Edward!"

Damon turned to see a portly man wearing a Savile Row custom-tailored suit approach. Bryant Bengtsson's dress was always impeccable, his white beard trimmed and his elegant moustache styled. Yet his booming voice and perpetual broad grin set people at ease.

He returned Bengtsson's hearty handshake. "Thank you for inviting me."

"Nonsense. You and that intriguing executive assistant of yours put together quite the proposal."

"Thank you, sir."

Bengtsson glared at him. "Stop with that 'sir' nonsense. It's Bryant or Bengtsson."

"Understood."

"Good." Bengtsson tossed back another drink and winced. "This stuff's potent. Need to pause if I'm going to keep my wits about me tonight. Will your executive assistant be attending tonight as well?"

Damon glanced at him as he maintained a neutral expression. He respected Bengtsson, but the older man was razor sharp and looking out for the best interests of his own company. He had no doubt the man was playing things casually to give Damon an opportunity to either say something witty or plant his foot firmly in his mouth.

"Yes."

"I was surprised to learn it was a temporary assistant who helped you." When Damon merely continued to look at him, Bengtsson chortled. "I'd like to play poker with you sometime." He signaled for a refill on his drink from a passing waiter. "It's not like you to trust someone with something this big. Speaking of," he continued as he slipped briskly from teasing trickster to efficient business mogul, "I'd like for you and Crowley's operations officer to stay after dinner. Consider it a cocktail hour to discuss the final steps in the selection process."

"Of course."

A flash of green drew his gaze to the stairs. His breath caught.

Evolet descended the stairs, a vision in a strapless dark green dress. The bodice was molded perfectly to her chest, the full skirt flaring out from her waist and covered in big white flowers. Her hair was pulled back from her face to show off her exquisite features before falling in gentle waves onto her shoulders.

She saw him and smiled. The nervousness in her eyes, the slight hesitation in her step as she glanced at the other guests before squaring her shoulders and continuing down, all of it made his heart thud harder against his ribs.

Bengtsson clapped him once on the back.

"Dinner will be served in fifteen minutes. And Edward?"

Damon tore his eyes away from Evolet long enough to meet Bengtsson's suddenly somber gaze.

"I've always been impressed with what Bradford Global has accomplished under your leadership." His eyes flicked toward Evolet. "Just don't let business blind you to other important things."

With those parting words, Bengtsson moved over to his wife. Damon turned to watch Evolet glide closer. When she reached his side, he took her hand in his and raised her fingers to his lips.

"You look beautiful."

"Thank you."

Her breathy voice washed over him and made his chest tighten. He plucked a champagne flute from a passing tray and handed it to her. They walked over to the stone wall that separated the private dining terrace from the plunge of the cliff down to the midnight waves of the ocean. Silver pinpoints of light dotted the sky.

"It's incredible," Evolet breathed.

"It is."

She glanced over at him, a shy smile tilting her lips up before she took a sip of champagne.

"No matter what happens, Damon, thank you. For all of this."

Another surprise, he reflected as they gazed out over the sea. Not receiving the Royal Air contract would be a harsh blow. But somewhere during the rush of the past three weeks, it had no longer become the focus of his life, no longer seemed a matter of life and death. And he had the woman at his side to thank for that.

Evolet rested her chin on her hands as she gazed out over the jungle below her. The warm water of the infinity pool lapped gently against her back. Somewhere in the foliage a bird let out a high-pitched squawk, followed by a series of chirps that made her smile.

During the day, the soaring trees draped in vines and steam rising from the greenery had appeared mystical, like something from a fairy tale. By night, with the trees draped in darkness and stars glistening overheard like a blanket of diamonds, the fairy tale had turned darker, more seductive.

She sighed, her eyes roaming over the landscape. Down below, lanterns flickered along the path that led to one of the resort's bars. A couple drifted down the stone walkway with their hands clasped tightly together. The man stopped, tugging his laughing companion back to him before he cupped the back of her head and kissed her.

Embarrassment heated Evolet's cheeks at observing the intimate moment. She pushed off the wall and floated on her back. Embarrassment and, she admitted with a wrinkle of her nose, longing.

Back in New York, there had been so many distractions to keep her from ruminating on the state of her relationship with Damon. But each night they spent together pulled at her, that thread she had used to tie her heart up unraveling at a rapid rate that both excited and frightened her. She had finally admitted to herself on the plane as she'd lain in his arms after they'd made love that she was falling—and falling hard. Perhaps it had been sparked that first night when he'd insisted on walking her through Central Park. Or maybe it had been seeing how well he treated his employees, how much he genuinely cared about their success as much as his company's.

Whatever had shifted her feelings, she needed to get them under control. A part of her hoped that something might change. But that hope needed to stay under lock and key. She would not force herself on Damon, wouldn't guilt him into something he didn't want.

Her chest rose and fell as she inhaled deeply. How many times had she indulged in hope as a child, thinking that perhaps she was arriving in what would be her last foster home? She had a sobering suspicion that she was repeating the same mistake now, ignoring the numerous warning signs that this affair was destined for only one place—heartbreak.

Perhaps when they got back to New York, she would spend a couple days in her own apartment. Since she and Damon had first made love, they'd been inseparable. She wouldn't be able to untangle herself from her emotions and prepare for the end of their affair if she didn't have a break.

It wasn't running away, she told herself. Not after what he'd told her on the plane. This was making a smart, informed decision of respecting his choices while protecting herself.

"You're thinking too hard."

She gasped and swallowed a mouthful of water. Sputtering, she stood up, whirled around and glared at him.

"Is your meeting with Bengtsson over?"

"Yes."

She frowned. "And?"

"And what?"

Her eyes narrowed. "Did Bengtsson say anything about the contract?"

"We'll know by Monday."

He walked toward the edge of the pool, each slow, methodical step kicking her heartbeat up a notch. It wasn't fair that he looked so damned handsome in tan slacks and a white linen shirt rolled up to his elbows. His eyes drifted down. Heat flared in his eyes as his body tensed. She looked down and saw the triangles of her bikini barely clinging to the globes of her breasts. Mortified, she sank down until the water came up to her neck.

He crouched down. "I've seen far more of you than that exquisite bikini covers."

She swallowed hard. "I'm aware."

His chuckle was a slow, sensual roll across her senses. He leaned down farther, and she found herself drifting toward him, her face upturned, her breathing unsteady. He stopped his mouth a breath away from hers, his lips curving up into a smile.

"Consider this payback for teasing me with that incredible dress tonight."

And then he pulled back. It took a moment for her brain to catch up to the fact that the bastard was taunting her. And damn it, he knew how much she wanted him to kiss her.

He chuckled again. Smug and self-assured. Her eyes narrowed. Impulse brought her hand up, her fingers fisting in the material of his shirt as she tugged. He tumbled into the infinity pool with a splash.

Evolet couldn't help herself—she laughed. She couldn't stop laughing as he stood, water dripping from the dark curls plastered to his forehead, his handsome face a dark glower. The laughter drifted away as she drank in the sight of his shirt clinging to his broad shoulders and the chiseled muscles of his stomach, the material translucent in the moonlight.

"It's not fair," she whispered.

"What?"

"You look like a damned underwear model."

"I have a personal trainer and a gym." He moved toward her, water rippling out from him as he drew near. "It helps me relax."

His arms circled her waist, his hands resting on her bare back. The feel of his skin against hers made her gasp and arch into him.

"You don't feel very relaxed right now."

He pressed his hips against hers, and her eyes widened, her body flooding with heat as she felt his growing hardness against her core.

"Damon…"

He stared down at her, his chest rising and falling, his breathing harsh. "I want you, Evolet."

Oh, yes, she was definitely in trouble. Her body grew heavy even as desire shimmered through her veins, made her breasts feel full and an ache start to hum deep inside her. But his erotic words didn't just inspire lust. No, they took those dratted feelings and fanned the flames into something far brighter and more dangerous.

Empowered and touched, she threaded her fingers through his hair and pulled his lips down to hers. Their mouths met, and she could swear the air rippled with the strength of the passion between them. He molded her body to his as he returned her kiss. He started off slowly, a firm press of his mouth against hers. Then a slow descent into something deeper as his tongue teased the seam of her lips until she laughed and opened for him.

The second their tongues met, the teasing disappeared. He growled and hauled her against him. She wrapped her legs around his waist, moaning as her back bowed, her breasts pressing against the wet material of his shirt.

Wildness seized her, and she reached back to undo her top. She wanted, *needed* to feel his chest against hers. But he reached up, caught her hand in his.

"Not yet. I like this, seeing you just barely covered." He nipped her earlobe with his teeth. "Knowing what's underneath." One hand tightened possessively on her rear. "Knowing I'm the only one who's seen you bare skinned, the only one who's been inside your glorious body."

The evocativeness of his words made her gasp right

before he kissed her again. This time he plundered, claimed, making love to her mouth as sensation built, tearing her in a dozen different directions as the ache between her thighs grew.

He scooped her up in his arms and moved to the edge of the pool. He set her on the edge, then kneeled in the water between her legs and settled his hands on her thighs. Shyness overtook her as his intent became clear.

He looked at her, then paused, rising up out of the water to cup her face with his hand. "We can stop."

She had been on the verge of asking him to pause, to let her catch her breath, to mentally prepare for placing herself in such a vulnerable position. His words banished her hesitation. She leaned forward and placed the softest of kisses on his mouth.

"Please don't," she whispered against his lips.

He returned her kiss, so light it could have been the whisper of butterfly wings on her flesh. He trailed his mouth down over her jawline, her neck, his tongue a molten flash of heat against her sensitive skin, then down over the exposed swells of her breasts. When his mouth closed over one nipple through the thin material, she cried out. He repeated the same heated caress on her other breast before kissing his way down her stomach and settling once more between her thighs.

He slowly pulled the wet material of her bikini bottoms to the side. Cool air kissed her thighs. His hands slid under her legs, pulling her closer to the edge of the pool. Closer to him.

And then his mouth was on her, kissing, licking, sucking, doing incredibly wicked things to her most sensitive skin. She could feel the sensation building, pulsing between her legs until she reached a fever pitch, as if her body were stretched so tight she might burst if something didn't happen, if he didn't do something to relieve ache that threatened to pull her under.

"Damon," she whimpered. "Damon, please."

One long caress with his tongue, one open-mouthed kiss to her most sensitive skin, and she came apart. Her body thrashed as she bowed up into the relentless heat of his mouth, her fingers grasping at his hair, his shoulders, anything to grab onto to steady her through the storm. She cried out his name, or at least she thought she did as her pleasure hit its pinnacle.

And then she slowly slid back onto the deck, her legs still draped wantonly over his shoulders. Ten minutes ago she would have been embarrassed. Now she was too sated, too limp to care.

"We should do that more."

He chuckled as he hauled himself up out of the pool and laid on the deck next to her. Before she could make another joke, something to help her heart stay strong against the tenderness settling over her like a warm blanket, he reached down and smoothed a strand of hair out of her face.

Her breath caught as tears pricked her eyes. The way he looked at her, with such gentleness, pulled that tenderness up from the heaviness of satisfied passion and brought it far too close to the surface.

Before she could say anything, he picked her up in his arms once more and carried her inside the villa. He carried her to his room and into his shower. He undressed her, then himself, tossing their soaking wet clothes into a pile on the floor. Each caress, each stroke of his hand, stoked her desire once more so that she was wet and panting when he slid inside her. He made love to her slowly against the wall of the shower, swallowed her cries with a kiss that burned itself into her heart.

As she drifted off that night, secure in the circle of his arms, an exciting and terrifying thought drifted through her mind.

If she wasn't in love with Edward Charles Damon Bradford, she was damned close.

CHAPTER FIFTEEN

DAMON STOOD AT the window of his office. The sun rose over New York City, casting a rosy golden glow on buildings that had stood for over a century, on new construction, on early morning commuters and joggers and tourists walking the maze of sidewalks, subway tunnels and avenues.

The city that never slept. He'd never been in his office early enough to see the sun rise, and now, seeing its beauty firsthand, he couldn't fathom why.

Even though he had arrived at a quarter till five in the morning, which would have put Bryant Bengtsson at just before five in the afternoon in Bali, to take the most important call of his career so far, he'd carved out an additional hour to watch the sun rise.

Because of Evolet. Because she had stood at the window and talked about how beautiful the sunrise must be on the city.

Like so many things, Evolet had made him see the city differently. He'd always prided himself on how he ran his company, the relationships he maintained with his employees. Yet work had ruled his life. She had made him stop so many times over the last few weeks, savor, relax, enjoy, like he never had.

And now…he cast a glance back at his desk, at the printout of the initial contract Bengtsson had sent over.

The contract naming Bradford Global as manufacturer of Royal Air's new fleet.

It meant something that his first reaction hadn't been pride in his company or satisfaction in the achievement of his employees. No, it had been excitement at the prospect of sharing with Evolet what their hard work had achieved.

Unsettled, he crossed the room to pick up the contract. Never had he wanted to share something so important with another person since his parents had passed. The most important thing in his life had been Bradford Global.

His rational side urged him to terminate their arrangement. She had become too significant far too quickly. His walls were coming down. He found himself anticipating not only their nights spent in his bed but what she would think about this decision, what witty remark she would have for him following a contentious meeting. He didn't just want sex.

He wanted her.

But the pleasure he found, both in bed and in her company, was coming at a price. They'd departed Bali and, with the time change, arrived in New York on Sunday morning. Evolet had been oddly quiet on the flight, opting to go back to her apartment when they'd landed and insisting she just wanted some time to decompress. He'd disliked how much he'd wanted her to stay, so he'd let her go. When he'd awoken in the night tangled in his sheets with sweat cooling on his skin and the imagined screams of his parents in their final moments echoing in his ears, he'd been grateful she hadn't been there to see his past rising up to claim him once more.

This was what happened when he let go of his control, when he entertained thoughts of his past and gave in to the craving for the woman who had become important to him. It had been years since he'd had a nightmare about the night his life had changed. He was perched on the edge of a very slippery slope.

He needed to step back.

A crackling sound drew his attention downward. The contract, now wrinkled, was clutched in his fingers. Slowly, he set it down, smoothed it out. He'd print off a new copy before anyone arrived.

With a heavy sigh, he sat in his chair and spun around again to watch the city come to life under the early morning light. The reasonable course of action was to end things with her. She'd told him that night on his balcony that one day she might want something more, a husband and a family of her own. He had opened up to her more than he had to anyone else since he'd lost his parents. But that didn't mean he was anywhere close to wanting a relationship. Evolet deserved to be with someone who could let himself feel without reservation, who could love her.

Except that every time he even contemplated the possibility of another man touching Evolet, to hear her whispered murmurings and have *his* name on her lips, Damon wanted to hurl his desk chair out the window.

No more.

It would hurt, yes, far more than he had expected when he'd first agreed to this insane arrangement. But it was for the best. He couldn't love and lose another person. He wasn't capable.

A weight pressed on his chest. He wanted to be capable. He wanted to be strong enough. For himself. For her. But what if he failed? What if he spiraled downward, back into that ugly hole he'd barely crawled out of the first time? A pit filled with anger and hate?

No. It wasn't worth the risk. Before Evolet, it had been about protecting his own heart.

But now…now it was about protecting her. About setting her free.

He had arranged a surprise for her for this weekend, either a conciliation getaway if they didn't receive the contract or a celebration if they did. One more weekend, and then they would go their separate ways.

It would be enough. It had to be enough.

Dimly, he heard the sound of heels clicking on the tile. He frowned and turned his head toward the door. Julie must be exceptionally early today. A surprise, given that he had seen her on several occasions before her morning coffee. The cheery side of her personality was decidedly enhanced by several shots of espresso.

A tentative knock sounded on the doorframe. He stood. "It's open."

The door opened, and his heart hammered into his chest. Evolet stood there in a voluminous red skirt and a navy shirt that hugged her breasts. A braid fell over one shoulder, tendrils curling to frame her face.

"Hi."

The simple greeting shot through him, not just with the sexual heat he'd come to expect around her but something deeper.

Longing. Longing to go to her, pick her up and swing her around the waist as he kissed her and told her the good news. He released a breath he hadn't even realized he'd been holding since his limo had dropped her off at her apartment and he'd watched her disappear inside the building, wondering if she was going to end their affair early.

Because, selfish bastard that he was, he wanted just a little more time.

He laid his hands on the desk, pressed his palms firmly against the cool surface. "Good morning."

She smiled shyly.

"I know it's early, I just…" Her eyes dropped down, then widened as she saw the crumpled contract on his desk. "Is that…" At his nod, she rushed into his office, around his desk and flung her arms around his neck.

"Oh, Damon, congratulations!" She kissed him, her enthusiasm teasing a smile from him. "I'm so happy for you. You must be so proud."

"I am."

She pulled back, her expression turning to one of confusion. "What's wrong?"

"Nothing." He dropped a quick kiss onto her forehead, then gently unwound her arms from his neck. "It's early, and it still hasn't fully settled in."

"Oh." Her cheeks turned pink. "I'm sorry, I shouldn't have…" She motioned to his mouth. "Kissed you. I know you said nothing in the office."

"It's all right." He leaned down, letting his smile widen. "We can celebrate properly this weekend. I'd like to take you somewhere."

She returned his smile with a cautious one of her own. "We just got back from Bali."

"This is much closer. Just us."

"I'd like that." She stared up at him, her eyes large and gold. "Are you sure you're all right?"

"Yes." To reassure her, he cast a quick glance at the door, then leaned down and pressed a lingering kiss to her lips. "See me again in a couple hours after I've had some coffee and recovered a bit more from jet lag. You won't be able to stop me from talking about it."

She returned his smile with a tentative one of her own. He didn't like it, didn't like her lack of a feisty comeback or a prim remark. She was worried about him. Worried because of how he was acting.

But he couldn't play nice. He had to prepare for the end, to handle this as he should have been handling it all along.

As she walked out, her skirt swinging back and forth like a bell, he told himself that it was for the best.

Now if only he could believe it.

Evolet forced herself to lean back into the seat of the limo. A red rose and a sparkling glass of champagne had awaited her, along with a friendly driver who had told her "Mr. Bradford" would meet her at the airport.

Her fingers drummed a nervous rhythm on the shining wood of the console. Was she analyzing his absence too much? Did it mean something, anything?

She sighed and took a fortifying sip of champagne. Riding the emotional roller coaster of the past week had once again reminded her of the ups and downs of her time in foster care. Getting comfortable, adjusted, making friends, only to be yanked away and shoved into another stranger's house, one who might be nice or one who tolerated her presence for the monthly check.

She glanced down at the little yellow suitcase resting at her feet. She'd packed, unpacked, then repacked at least a half a dozen times.

What, she had mused more than once, did one pack for a celebration weekend away with one's lover-not-boyfriend?

It had taken a glass of wine to summon enough courage to pack the lingerie she'd picked up with her bonus check at a pricey boutique in the Upper West Side.

Just a week ago, she would have packed it without a second thought. But she'd spent the past four nights alone. On Tuesdays, traveling from the church in Harlem where she practiced with the Apprentice Symphony back down to Midtown didn't make sense. But Monday, Wednesday and Thursday, Damon had had late meetings, dinner with his administrative team and other excuses he'd delivered with a coolness that reminded her of how he'd been toward the end of their dance at the gala fundraiser.

A stark difference from the weeks before when it had seemed like Damon hadn't wanted to be apart from her. Dinners, trips to museums and parks, waking up to find him pressed against her. Even though he hadn't been able to say the words, the way he'd treated her had made her wonder if there was something more. That perhaps he was starting to feel something for her.

But things between them had changed drastically. Gone was the warm camaraderie, the relaxed pleasure they'd found in each other's company. Had she made Damon feel suffocated, allowed too much of her own emotions to show through? Is that what had prompted the conversation on the airplane? Or was he simply tiring of her?

Stop it.

She'd played these mind games with herself before,

always wondering what she could have done differently to make a foster family care more, make them consider adopting her. In reality, there had been nothing she could've done.

Just as there was nothing she could do right now, except enjoy what time she had left with Damon. Whether or not he felt anything for her was irrelevant as long as he held on to his belief that he was incapable of love or a relationship.

A rational conclusion. Too bad her heart preferred to cling to irrational hope.

She traced a finger over the velvety rose petals. Not spending the evenings with him had been a good wake-up, though, that she had spent far too much time with him. She'd used the nights to return to a schedule similar to the one of her former life. Her life before Damon. If it suddenly felt a little emptier, a little lonelier than it had before, well, she'd adjust. She'd keep going, just like she always did.

Satisfaction slipped in and eclipsed some of her moodiness. She'd become invested in seeing Bradford Global succeed, more so than any organization she'd worked for. Being an executive assistant would never replace her own passions and goals. But it had been the first time in a long time that she'd let herself care about anything other than her music and Constanza.

Still, she had tried to focus on the positives of the nights to herself. Monday and Wednesday had been spent in the park practicing and taking photos and videos for her social media accounts. Tuesday had been her weekly session with the Apprentice Symphony. This time, when her section leader had invited her to join the others for a drink, she'd said yes. And, she reflected with a small smile, she'd had a great time.

By Thursday, she hadn't spoken with Damon privately since that brief moment in his office at the beginning of the week. She'd barely even seen him at work aside from passing him in the hall or glimpsing him in a meeting in one of the glass-enclosed conference rooms.

When her phone had pinged at six o'clock Thursday night, her heart had started to pound frantically against her ribs when she'd seen his name on her screen. His text had been short, telling her a limo would pick her up the following evening and take her to the airport. It had taken her twelve minutes to come up with her brilliant reply—See you then—before she'd run around the apartment like a maniac.

All to pack one small suitcase that hopefully made it look like she'd artlessly tossed a few things together and waltzed out the door.

The limo turned into a small heliport next to the river. Her breath escaped in a whoosh. She had no idea what to expect. If Damon was as cool and distant as he had been Monday, would she be able to enjoy the weekend? If he greeted her with the same chaste kiss he'd bestowed upon her in his office, would it be better to tell him she changed her mind and have the limo take her home?

She'd taken the tags off the lingerie, she thought with a grimace as the limo stopped next to a sleek black helicopter. Oh, well. If she went home, she could slip into the scarlet teddy, pour herself a glass of wine and watch spy movies in luxurious silk.

Damon walked around the helicopter, his face

turned up toward the rotor blades, his body silhouetted against the backdrop of dusk in New York City. She stared at him from behind the tinted window, drinking in every detail. The sharp jut of his chin, the broadness of his shoulders, the wind ruffling his thick hair.

Steeling herself for whatever was to come, she lifted her chin and started to open the door, only to find her hand brushing air as the limo driver opened it for her.

"Welcome to the Harbor Heliport, ma'am."

"Thank you. And thank you for the ride, too, Adam."

She turned and nearly melted at the smile Damon shot at her as he loped across the tarmac to her side.

"Hi." He took her hand in his and brushed a kiss across her knuckles that made her breath catch.

"Hi," she replied.

His grip tightened on hers as he nodded toward the helicopter. "Are you ready?"

She breathed in deeply. She would enjoy the weekend, enjoy her time with Damon, however much she had left. No regrets.

She looked at him, smiled and squeezed his hand. "I'm ready."

The helicopter ride was a wondrous experience. It was incredibly sexy watching Damon manage the controls, forearms flexing as he expertly flew first over the city and did a quick circle around the Statue of Liberty before turning the helicopter north. As the city gave way to suburbs and then long, beautiful stretches of ocean to the right and the coastline to the left, he played both the role of pilot and tour guide. An hour flew by in the blink of an eye.

And then the house appeared. The sun clung to the pine trees and gave enough light to show the Bradford Estate at its finest. Golden-brown cedar shingles stood out against white trim. Evolet counted at least four porches, five balconies and one stunning staircase off the back that descended onto a green lawn. Beyond the retaining wall, a sandy beach beckoned along the banks of the Hudson River.

Once he'd landed and secured the helicopter, he grasped her hand in his and escorted her inside. The interior was equally incredible. Unlike his company's headquarters, cozy with its dark colors and plush leather furniture, here the chairs were cream trimmed in blue, the walls a mix of white wood and red brick and the art vivid paintings and photographs of the ocean and nearby town.

Eventually they ended upstairs in the primary bedroom, complete with a white four-poster king-sized bed piled high with fluffy pillows and a veranda that overlooked the river. She moved to the balcony doors and gazed out over the rolling, tree-covered slopes of the Catskill Mountains.

"This is beautiful, Damon." She glanced over her shoulder at him and smiled. "Thank you."

He moved behind her, his arms circling around her waist. She sighed and leaned into his embrace. Her hands settled over his. He stiffened, the movement so quick she wondered if she'd imagined it.

Before she could analyze it, he turned her around and pressed his lips to hers. She circled her arms around his neck, moaning into his mouth as his hands moved over her body with a lover's intimate knowledge. They stripped each other of clothing, their movements almost frantic, as if they both needed the comfort of each other's touch. He laid her down, then covered her body with his own. She slipped her fingers into his hair and tried to tug him down for another kiss, but he evaded her, trailing his lips down her neck and over her breasts, stopping to suck first one nipple and then the other into his mouth. By the time he reached her most intimate skin, she was trembling, begging. He teased her with gentle kisses and little nips of his teeth before placing his mouth over her. She arched into him, cried out as she shuddered with her release.

When he slipped inside her, she wrapped her arms around him, savored every stroke as they moved together, climbing higher until she called out his name and crested. He followed a moment later, his groan of satisfaction reverberating throughout her body.

Yet as they lay together, she couldn't help but notice that he didn't press a kiss to her forehead, didn't let his hand drift down to rest possessively on her stomach. Even though he relaxed right next to her, she felt the distance between them widen a fraction more.

CHAPTER SIXTEEN

THE PLATES GLEAMED on top of silver chargers. A lone red rose stood proud in a glass bud vase, the petals unfurled so perfectly it could have been captured in a photograph. A light wind blew in off the river and made the flames of the votive candles flicker. The scent of clams steamed in butter, white wine and garlic wafted from one of the silver-covered platters on the side table.

It was perfect.

So why, Damon mused as he shoved his hands into his pockets and stood at the edge of the balcony, *do I feel hollow?*

They'd spent most of Saturday in the house, curled up in front of a roaring fire as a morning spring rain had chilled the air outside. They'd made love on the rug before lunch, then again in the lavish bed after. She was like a drug in his system. If she wasn't in the room, he was wondering where she was. If she was by his side, he was contemplating how soon would be too soon to take her into his arms again.

Then there had been the library. The rain had continued through the afternoon. He'd shown her the library, an enchanting room with gleaming pine bookshelves that stretched up nearly twenty feet, plump cream-colored chairs and couches that encouraged one to sink into their depths and read. Evolet had picked a mystery, he a science-fiction epic, and they had sunk down onto the couch, reading with her legs draped across his knees as the rain pattered softly on the windows.

There had been no heat, no foreplay, no sex. They'd simply existed together in mutual contentment. She'd practiced her cello after dinner before the fire. Had she noticed the difference in her own playing, he wondered, or was he imagining it himself? The newfound sensualness of how she held the cello between her thighs, the confidence in her hands as she drew the bow across the strings? Every move had been amplified, every note ringing with passion instead of the sadness he'd heard the night of the fundraiser, the bitterness of regret and loss when she'd played for him in his office.

Part of him wanted to end things now. He'd thought this weekend would be enough—one last fling before ending it.

Just one more night.

He refocused on the moment at hand. His grandfather had picked an incredible spot to build his retreat. The river sparkled like a jewel as the sun slowly sank behind the mountains to the west. Red oak and sugar maple trees jutted proudly from the slopes and rises of the Catskills. Bursting with green leaves, they would turn in the autumn to burgundy, orange and amber, a rich display that set the hills on fire.

He wanted to ask Evolet to come back with him, to lie with him under a blanket on the balcony and gaze out over the river, then turn to each other as darkness settled and the air turned cool.

His fingers curled into fists. He'd known from the

moment she'd stepped out of the limo and onto the tarmac at the helipad that he was risking far too much by indulging in this weekend with her. But God help him, he'd been too weak to resist.

The same weakness that whispered to him that this could continue beyond tomorrow. That they could continue this affair and he could bring her back with him in the fall.

No.

He was fortunate he hadn't a repeat of the nightmare he'd experienced when they'd returned from Bali, although he attributed that to reclaiming the reigns he normally held tightly on his control. Another example of how opening himself up would only lead to trouble.

He had never been vulnerable to another human being after his parents had died. He'd wrapped himself up in work, used it to help him focus and eventually move on from their deaths. Each success of Bradford Global had brought respite, had healed him as he worked to preserve his family's legacy, to honor his father's memory and the trust his father had placed in his son. Numbers, contracts, output—these were tangible results, ones achieved with the right initiative, hard work. Measurable results that kept him grounded.

Emotion offered no such stability. The slightest indulgence of feelings opened the door to the utter loss, the bone-deep grieving that had threatened to render him catatonic in the days after the accident.

Emotion could be incredible, a high unlike any other.

It could also spell doom, pulling one into a pit so deep it would be almost impossible to climb out of.

He'd barely clawed himself out of depression before. He couldn't risk being on the brink of such loss again.

More importantly than that, Evolet deserved better than what he could give. In the weeks they'd been together, she'd blossomed. How long could she keep growing, keep rising above her own pains and insecurities if all he did was drag her back down into the dark?

A sailboat rounded the bend, white fabric billowing under the spring breeze as it sailed between the two falls of mountains that sloped down to the river. Damon watched the boat, remembered the look of sheer pleasure on Evolet's face as he'd taken her out on the speedboat this afternoon, watched her hair whip in the breeze as she'd taken the wheel and laughed.

Yes, it was best to follow the original plan and end things tomorrow on their way back to New York City. He would have memories of this weekend, of their mind-blowing affair and the incredible gift she had given him to warm him in the coming months and years.

The rational pep talk did little to soothe the tempest churning inside his chest.

He knew the moment she stepped onto the balcony even though she hadn't made a sound. He breathed in deeply, steadied himself and turned.

And felt like fate punched him in the gut.

She stood framed in the doorway, her hair tumbling over bare shoulders in loose waves. Vivid red clung to her torso, strips of material wrapped around her arms like a lover's hands, while the skirt flared out and down to her knees. Her feet were bare, an erotic contrast to the romantic sweetness of her dress.

"Hi."

After the many times they'd made love, after they'd
tasted each other, she could still sound breathless like
she was seeing him for the first time. Her eyes sparkled like the tiny diamonds at her ears, the only jewelry she wore.

"Good evening."

He stepped forward, took her hand and escorted her
to her seat. Everything he did—filling her bowl with
clams and placing a thick slice of crispy baguette on
her plate, pouring a glass of sparkling white wine—
brought a charmed smile or a soft flare of excitement
to her eyes.

It was, he realized as the sun continued its descent
and set her golden hair aglow with rays of red and
orange, one of the things he enjoyed most about her.
How much she delighted in the little things, from
the spinning of the carousel in Central Park to him
cooking her breakfast. As much as he had tried to
stay grounded as Bradford Global had grown by leaps
and bounds, he had grown used to the luxury, the
opulence afforded one with millions of dollars at his
fingertips.

Dessert was a decadent chocolate mousse topped
with fresh whipped cream. Afterward, they reclined
in their chairs and watched the stars appear in the vel-
vet darkness.

"The perfect weekend," Evolet said on a soft sigh.

"It is." Damon leaned forward and clinked his glass
to hers. If he could just focus on what they had enjoyed,
on the time they'd spent together and not the inevitable
end, he would get through this evening without making a fool of himself.

"Damon…"

The hint of melancholy in her voice pulled at him. She stared out over the river, her profile lit with the silver wash of moonlight. Slowly, she turned to look at him.

"Make love to me."

Did he imagine the slight catch in her voice? The emotion in her eyes? It called to him, seduced him.

Then he pushed it away.

Of course she feels something, he told himself as he rose.

He was her first lover. She confided in him, yes, pushed him to share more of himself with her. But she hadn't said a word about how she felt about him, about continuing their affair beyond her contract time at Bradford Global. Perhaps he was more conflicted than she.

The thought should have brought him comfort. Instead, it just left him empty.

He moved to her and swept her into his arms, cradling her body close. He carried her inside. They undressed each other with gentle, languorous movements, savoring each other's bodies until they lay naked on the bed. When he pressed his body into hers, felt the arch of her hips against his as he claimed her with slow strokes, he almost asked her to stay. When her nails dug into his back and she cried out his name as she came apart in his arms, he almost told her he felt something, more than anything he'd ever felt for a woman.

And as she lay in his embrace, her breathing deep and even, he kissed her brow and acknowledged that Evolet Grey had, for better or worse, changed his life.

* * *

Evolet had always pictured hell as being a place of fire
and brimstone, wails of grief and gnashing of demon
teeth.

She'd never pictured it as the black concrete of a
helipad rushing up to meet the landing skids of a helicopter. But as Damon expertly maneuvered the helicopter down, as she felt the slight bump signaling that
they had landed, her heart shuddered.

When she'd woken this morning, it had been to an
empty bed. And when she'd walked down the stairs,
Damon had been wearing a crisp white dress shirt and
navy pants, a black belt notched at his lean waist and an
expensive watch glinting in the light as he'd sipped a
cup of coffee and scrolled through emails on his tablet.

He'd looked up at her, smiled. But it had been a dull
smile, one she imagined he reserved for placating an-
noying business partners or one-night stands who over-
stayed their welcome.

And then, as she'd poured herself a cup, he'd said it.

*I've enjoyed our time together, Evolet. But it's time
for us to go our separate ways.*

The roaring in her ears had drowned out most of
what he'd said, although she'd caught something about
how he'd wanted to tell her here, in private, in case
there was anything they needed to discuss.

She'd said no, plastered a smile on her face and excused herself to go pack. She'd discovered that crying
her heart out in the shower had its benefits, like the
stream of the water covering up her sobs. She had suspected this might be coming sooner rather than later.
All through the weekend there had been a distance to

him, as if he'd been trying to make the time into what she had originally proposed: a quick fling.

She just hadn't expected him to end it like this, before they'd even headed back to the city.

The quick bout of tears helped her steady herself before she'd gone back down. He'd looked at her then, his eyes running over her as if searching for signs that she was about to break. She'd merely lifted her chin up and asked if he was ready.

Falling in love with him had been her own choice. One day, hopefully sometime soon, she would be grateful for all he'd shown her, for helping her realize she could still love even if she knew pain would follow.

But not today. Today was for mourning.

The flight back to New York had been stilted. The camaraderie and fun conversation that had filled their journey to the river valley was nonexistent on the ride back. She'd kept herself distracted with a book, her eyes only occasionally flickering to his hands as he'd maneuvered the controls or to his handsome profile while he'd gazed out over the scenery below them.

And now, she thought as the helicopter blades slowed above them and several helipad employees rushed forward, it was over. Three days gone in the blink of an eye.

Her one meager suitcase was moved to the trunk of another limo parked at the edge of the helipad. She removed her cello case herself and carefully set it inside.

She turned to see Damon walking around the helicopter, talking to one of the employees as he gestured toward the tail of the helicopter. It was still morning, the sun gathering force from the encroaching summer season and shining its full heat down on the city. A bead of sweat trickled down the back of her.

He turned and smiled at her, a flash of white against his tan skin. Hope bubbled in her chest as he walked over to her.

"So…" He glanced at the limo. "You're ready?"

The hope burst, leaving her adrift.

"I am."

They stood no more than a couple feet apart. Yet she felt an ocean separating them, deep and dark and churning with secrets that would never be revealed.

Why, she suddenly thought. *Why can't we just talk about this? What if he feels something, too, and is just doing what I did, shoving the emotions away to keep the pain at bay?*

But the thought was banished as soon as she looked up. He was cold, the same unapproachable mask he'd wielded in the meeting she'd walked into all those weeks ago. In that moment she knew that if she were to give voice to her heart, he'd reject her.

He held out his hand. Hurt sliced through her, so sharp she had to bite back a gasp. How had the incredible passion, the beautiful moments they'd shared come down to this? A handshake when just last night he'd kissed the pulse beating at her throat, the slopes of her breasts, her lips as he'd joined his body with hers?

But this was how it had always been fated to end, she reminded herself. She'd proposed it. Damon had agreed to it. She had no reason to be upset.

She squared her shoulders, mentally prepared herself, and clasped his hand in one quick, businesslike shake.

"Thank you, Mr. Bradford." She inclined her head. "Have a good week."

With those mundane parting words hanging in the air, she turned and walked away from Damon Bradford.

The only man she'd ever loved.

CHAPTER SEVENTEEN

EVOLET LEANED AGAINST the cool wall of the subway platform, her eyes drifting up to the marquee with the arrival times. A train rushed by, a blur of light and faces, before it disappeared back into the dark.

A sigh escaped her. It had been three weeks since Damon had ended their affair. One week since she'd walked out the doors of Bradford Global for the last time. She'd technically had one week left on her contract, but the Monday after their final weekend, she'd arrived at work to find that Damon had taken himself on a tour of Bradford Global's manufacturing facilities. She'd managed to power through the following two weeks, wrapping up the mundane list of tasks and busy work he had left with speedy efficiency. By the end of the first week, she'd knocked out everything. By the end of the second week, after seeking out work from several departments and spending most of her afternoons twiddling her thumbs, she'd reached out to her agency, who had arranged for her contract to end early due to "assigned work being completed." Her agency had also approved a two-week sabbatical. Time for her to breathe, to relax.

To heal.

Walking out on her last day had been painful. But it had been necessary.

She'd filled the last week with practice sessions in the park, visits to Constanza and far too many lattes at a roastery at the southern edge of East Harlem. Not to mention the two glasses of wine she'd imbibed last night as she'd sat on the fire escape of her apartment and soaked in the symphony of her neighborhood—the raucous honks of taxis and shrill shriek of sirens, the lilting phrases of Spanish, Creole and French drifting up from the sidewalks.

Escapism. Yet the nutty, caramelized scent of Italian roasted espresso, the sound of birds chirping in the background as she'd wrung heartbreak from her cello in Central Park, the dark taste of the merlot she'd sipped as she'd gazed up at the moon had all given her what she needed to survive having a broken heart.

The first day, every time her phone had pinged she'd forced herself to wait one minute, two, three before she'd picked it up with a tremor she wished she could deny but didn't. And every text, every notification had all had one thing in common.

None of them had been from Damon.

By day two, she'd cried more than enough tears. By day three, she'd accepted that he wasn't going to contact her.

It had been so tempting to shut down again. And for a couple days she had. But then Tuesday had rolled around. She'd forced herself to say yes again to pizza after practice with the Apprentice Symphony. She'd even invited another cellist, Ashley, to join her in the park that weekend, where they'd practiced and filmed videos for their social media. She had booked several independent performances through her website and, hopefully, would land an audition or two in the coming weeks.

Slowly, day by day, she was coming to accept that her affair with Damon had brought about some very good changes. Good change didn't mean the pain was gone. Her chest still ached. When she closed her eyes at night, Damon's face rose in her mind. But each day was getting a little better. And, most importantly, she wasn't going to allow herself to crawl into a hole of regret. Her time with Damon had been incredible. To focus on the aftermath instead of the miracles of pleasure that had occurred would only be hurting herself.

A mechanical voice broke through her thoughts as it announced the train that would take her to her new assignment for a fancy law firm in downtown Brooklyn was just four minutes away. Another subway barreled down the tracks in the center of the station, the wheels groaning as the cars carried hordes of Monday-morning commuters squished inside like sardines. Wind kicked up in her face, and she glanced away from the tracks.

Just in time to see Audrey Clark from Bradford Global rush through the turnstile.

"Evolet!"

Her resolve splintered and nearly collapsed as Audrey rushed forward, curls bouncing and tumbling over her shoulders in time to her energetic steps. She enveloped Evolet in a hug.

"What are you doing here?" Audrey asked with a laugh as she stepped back.

"I live just a couple blocks from here."

"I didn't know that. Some of the cafés and restaurants up here are so much fun. And that garden shop under the bridge was such a surprise!"

Evolet listened to Audrey chatter, soaking up the sound of a familiar voice, the relaxed nature of inane conversation with someone whose company she enjoyed.

"I'm glad you like it up here. Were you up here just for fun?"

Audrey's smile widened. "I was on Saturday night. Then I met someone, and Saturday turned into Sunday and Sunday turned into…well, now." She grasped her hands together and sighed. "She made me breakfast. I've never stayed the night with someone and had them make me breakfast the next day. I think it means something."

The rest of Evolet's resolve crumpled into a shattered mess in her chest, jagged shards that cut deep. Would she ever be able to eat pancakes again without thinking of green eyes and hot hands roaming over her body with the assured confidence of a lover who knew her body as intimately as she knew her own?

"Hey." Audrey laid a hand on Evolet's shoulder, her brow creased with worry. "Are you okay?"

"Yeah." She forced a smile as she scrambled to come up with something before opting for as close to the truth as possible. "I was just remembering when someone made me breakfast after…well, you know."

"Sex," Audrey said with another laugh as Evolet blushed. "I do know."

"I think it means something, too."

"I hope so. I really like her. We have another date tomorrow night. But," Audrey added with a probing gaze, "I'm guessing the one who made you breakfast didn't do the smart thing and hold on to you."

"No, he didn't, but that's in the past." She squeezed Audrey's hand, her smile this time genuine. "Today is about you and someone who made you breakfast and who might turn out to be very special."

Audrey returned the squeeze. "I miss you, Evolet. We should get coffee. And by that I mean actually get coffee, not say we will and then never do."

She laughed. "I'd like that."

"Have you ever thought about quitting the agency and coming to work for us full-time?"

"I liked it a lot, but no. I need something with flexibility that will let me perform with my orchestra and go to my auditions."

"I bet Damon would be flexible with you," Audrey said, nearly making Evolet choke on a pained laugh. "He seemed to really like your work. You made a big impact on us getting the Royal Air contract."

Evolet's phone pinged, and she grabbed it, thankful to have a reason to look away before her emotions became visible in her eyes and betrayed her.

"Oh! Which reminds me…"

The sound of Audrey's voice faded as Evolet read the subject line of an email, then reread it again. Cautious hope bloomed in her chest, followed by a swift, all-encompassing joy.

"Evolet? Evolet, is everything okay?"

She looked up, her lips parted in shock. "I have an audition with the Emerald City Philharmonic. Today."

Audrey squealed and threw her arms around her. "Evolet, that's fantastic!"

"Thank you. I…" She was certain if she looked

away, if she blinked, the email would disappear. "I can't believe it. I sent in my audition video months ago and never heard, but someone canceled and I… I have an audition!" she finished gleefully as she returned Audrey's hug, suddenly and fervently grateful that she wasn't alone, that she had someone to share this moment with her.

I wish Damon were here.

She squelched that thought. He wasn't here. But Audrey was, and she would tell Constanza as soon as she got out of the station. She needed to call Miranda, too, have her find someone else to cover the first day at the law firm. She hated to do it, but this audition was too important to risk.

She glanced at her watch. It was still early. Perhaps if she went down to the firm in person, spoke with them directly and explained the situation, she could smooth any ruffled feathers while Miranda found a replacement.

"Well, that answers my question about the party."

"Party?" Evolet looked up then. "What party?"

"The party Damon's hosting tonight for everyone at Bradford Global. To celebrate the Royal Air contract."

Pain lanced through her, sharp and hot. She'd known—of course she'd known—that things were over. But it still hurt to not be invited, not after the credit Damon had given her. Just one more time she had started to feel like a part of things, to let down her guard and let herself care, only to have it taken away.

"Surely Damon invited you."

"It doesn't matter," Evolet replied breezily. "The audition's at six and—"

Her phone rang as her train pulled into the station.

She glanced down at the screen and frowned. Why would Samuel be calling her on a Monday? Fear bubbled in her stomach.

"Samuel?"

His sob made her go cold.

"Samuel? What is it? Where is she?"

"Hospital," he gasped out. "Evolet, she fell and they couldn't—"

"Which hospital?" she demanded as she turned and ran for the stairs. Audrey called out to her, but she couldn't think, couldn't stop to explain. As she ran up the stairs and into the light, frantically searching for a taxi, her heart pounded so hard she could barely breathe. She couldn't lose her, couldn't lose someone else, so soon.

Please, Constanza, just hold on. I'm coming.

The harsh scent of antiseptic mixed with burnt coffee and wilting flowers. A bland voice paged a doctor over the intercom as someone wept uncontrollably. Damon hadn't been in a hospital since that night twelve years ago, but the smells and sounds didn't change.

He stalked down the hall to the nurse's station. Fear tangled with indecision, which set him further on edge. He never questioned himself, didn't hesitate. If he made a mistake, he would examine it, find the flaws, note the successes and never repeat it again.

But now, as the cool-faced nurse looked up Constanza George's room number, he had never felt so conflicted. When Audrey had called him spouting off about Evolet, his first reaction had been instant longing, a need spreading like lightning through his body at the mere mention of her name. It had shifted from heat to ice instantly as Audrey had told him about what she'd overheard at 116th Street station.

I should have been there.

The thought pulsed through him, digging its insidious claws into his heart a little deeper each time. How many times had he pulled his phone out, started typing out a text message inviting her to the party, asking if she'd had any auditions, checking on Constanza…?

Anything and everything that would give him just one more chance to talk with her.

He'd screwed up at the heliport. He'd known as soon as he'd held out his hand. For God's sake, he'd taken her virginity, and he'd ended the most sensual, erotic, emotional affair of his life by shaking her damned hand?

It had been the act of a coward. He'd seen the indecision on her face, the faint hint of an emotion so deep and raw in her tawny gold eyes it had both thrilled and paralyzed him. Thrilled him because no one had ever looked at him like that. Paralyzed him because he had realized that she felt something for him, something more than just simple affection. He'd wanted it, wanted it so badly he had nearly asked her to go back with him to his penthouse, for them to find a way to make this work.

The possibility of what they could have—and lose— had scared him. So he'd made a decision in the heat of the moment.

The wrong one. One he'd been regretting since the emotion had winked out of her eyes and she'd coolly shaken his hand, turned and walked away without a backward glance. Taking a tour of the manufacturing facilities the following two weeks had been a logical step, and one that had thankfully given them space.

Coming back and learning that she had left a week early had cemented his conclusion. He'd screwed up. Bad.

But had he fixed his mistake? No, he'd just done what he'd done the first time he'd experienced such a devastating loss. He'd thrown himself into work the past week, sometimes staying the night at his office. More than once he'd woken up and reached for her, his fingers brushing empty space.

If he hadn't been a coward, she would have called him this morning when her world had started to fall apart. He could have been there for her so she didn't have to face the potential of loss alone again.

God, could he have been any more an idiot to let her walk away?

"Are you family?" the nurse asked, breaking through his mental self-flagellation.

"No, but—"

"Only family," she intoned, dismissing him as she looked at something on her computer.

"I'm not officially family, but—"

"Official is all we deal with around here," she replied with an arched eyebrow.

He fought back the sudden insane urge to laugh. All the times he had wanted to be treated like just a regular guy on the streets instead of a billionaire. Now, of all the times for his wish to be granted, it had to be when he needed to be by Evolet's side. And Constanza's. He'd never met Evolet's adoptive mother. The thought of never meeting the woman who'd rescued Evolet from her life of solitude, who had introduced her to music and family made his stomach twist so tightly it nearly made him sick.

"Look… Katelyn," he said as he glanced down at the nurse's name tag, "I need to see Constanza. She's very important to someone I…"

His voice trailed off. How could he describe how he felt about Evolet? How much she meant to him? How he needed to be with her if she lost the one person she had in the world who hadn't let her down?

"I don't know what happened today, but I need to see her in case…" His voice faltered as he remembered running through the hospital, past the crying and the muffled conversations and the steady beat of monitors, only to be confronted with a wall of silence in the room his mother had been taken to. Silence except for the dull thudding of his heartbeat as he'd stared at her bruised and broken body on the hospital bed.

The nurse's expression relaxed a fraction.

"Sir, I'm sorry. Truly," she added with a gentle pat on the back of his hand. "I can talk to her kids and ask, but—"

"Damon?"

Evolet's voice rolled over him, soft and roughened from crying. She stood in the middle of the hallway, blond curls falling out of her ponytail, her eyes rimmed in red and her face pale. Her arms were wrapped around her waist, as if she were comforting herself from whatever she'd just come from.

His heart catapulted into his throat. "Constanza?"

Evolet let out a shuddering breath. "She's going to

be okay. She fell and hit her head. She's a little disoriented, but so far all of the tests are coming back okay."

She spoke as if she were far away. Which she was, he realized with a spurt of panic as she didn't move, didn't flinch as a doctor rushed by and brushed her shoulder. She just stared at a point over his shoulder, her eyes blank. Only six feet away, but she might as well have been on the other side of the world.

"How are you?"

Her eyes shifted to him then. He waited to see something, a flicker of emotion, a flare of feeling.

"I'm here."

To hell with being careful.

He moved forward and pulled her into his arms, enfolding her in a tight embrace. His breath rushed out as her familiar scent washed over him, clean and sweet. Three weeks since he'd woken up to her in his bed, since he'd drawn her into his arms and kissed her like it was the last time he ever would.

It felt like a lifetime.

"Thank you for coming, Damon."

She didn't relax into his arms, didn't rest her head on his shoulder. She stayed stiff as a board for one long, drawn-out moment before planting a hand on his chest and gently but firmly pushing him away.

Don't! he wanted to shout. *Don't push me away.*

But he had no right to ask that of her. Especially right now, when tucking herself safely behind that wall of ice was probably the only thing keeping her on her feet.

"Don't worry about costs, Evolet, I'll—"

"No!"

He blinked at her vehement denial. Color rushed back into her cheeks, burning a hot pink as her eyes suddenly glittered with what he recognized as anger.

"This isn't your problem, Damon. It's mine and Samuel's."

"Don't be a fool," he replied, keeping his voice even. "I can make sure she receives the best of care and—"

"I'm her daughter," Evolet retorted. "It's my responsibility."

He paused, tried another tactic. "Audrey said right before Samuel called you got an audition with the Philharmonic. Are you going to give up on that, too?"

"It was for tonight. I can't leave her."

"Call the orchestra and tell them what happened."

"It's not like taking sick leave at work. There's one semi-final audition date, and today is it."

He didn't miss the slight crack in her voice, watch as she pulled herself back together and tried to yank the emotionless mask back in place.

"So what? You're going to bury yourself in medical debt and spend your best years working to pay it off instead of going after your dream? You think that's what Constanza wants for you?"

"You don't know her." Evolet's whisper came fiercely, adamantly. "And you don't know me, Damon. Don't act like you know what's important to me."

His hold on his temper began to slip. "If you need to use me as a punching bag, fine. But," he added as he closed the distance between them once more, stopping so his body was just a breath away from hers, "don't you stand there and say I don't know you. I know you better than anyone."

Her chin came up, eyes blazing. "We had sex. That's it. Over and done."

Perhaps this was the punishment he deserved after his casual liaisons, the coldness he'd wielded like a weapon to keep previous lovers at bay. The savage decisiveness he'd used when ending his affair with Evolet. Had his past partners experienced the powerless pressure of shock, the swift anger that raced up the spine, only to peter out into a desperate hopelessness that left one empty?

"Is that all we were, Evolet?" He leaned down, knowing he should leave, that now was not the time or place to be having this discussion. "You asked me to be your first lover."

"Lovers implies love. We didn't love each other. We had an agreement. We had fun. We had sex. Now it's over."

But I do love you.

The realization hit him hard. He was in love with Evolet. It stunned him into silence. He couldn't say it now, not in the midst of so much fear and pain, not when she was so angry and might not believe him. Not when she had every reason to doubt him with how he'd kept her at arm's length even as he'd greedily taken everything she'd offered.

Had she been in love with him? He was certain she had at least cared for him. But she had told what had happened the times she had loved and lost. She'd shut down, withdrawn so deeply into herself it had been years until she'd finally opened her heart again. Would there ever come a time when she would believe him? Or had he lost his chance?

"Go away, Damon," she said suddenly, weariness

creeping into her voice as her shoulders slumped. "You shouldn't even be here. You have your party tonight."

He hadn't just made one mistake or two. No, he had to have made at least a dozen where Evolet was concerned. She had been a crucial part of landing the Royal Air contract. Her passionate defense of Bradford Global and the work they did had meant something to Bryant Bengtsson. He'd almost invited her to the party half a dozen times over the past week, each time coming up with excuses that in retrospect were ungrateful and cowardly. Chief among them had been that he knew if he invited her, it was admitting that he wanted more from her than just a brief affair. He hadn't wanted to make himself vulnerable, hadn't wanted to risk showing his hand.

"Evolet—"

"Please." Her plea cut him so deeply he wondered if he'd ever heal. "Please, Damon. Just go, and don't think of me again."

He wanted nothing more than to go to her again, to draw her into his arms and stroke her hair, her back until she melted against him and laid her cheek over his heart as she sighed. He wanted to carry her to his bed and curl up with her under the covers and hold her through the night.

He wanted everything she couldn't give him right now. His very presence hurt her.

Love, he realized, didn't always mean getting to be with the one you wanted. Sometimes it meant walking away.

So he did, without another word or a backward glance at the woman he had loved and lost.

CHAPTER EIGHTEEN

EVOLET LEANED HER forehead against the cool glass of the hospital window. The morning sun that had taunted her when she'd burst out of the subway this morning, bright and warm as she'd gone cold with fear, was now buried behind dark gray clouds that eclipsed the tops of New York's skyline. Lightning forked across the sky, a brief flash of brilliance, followed by a very angry grumble of thunder.

It was almost as if she'd summoned the weather with her own foul mood. Once the last of the tests had come back negative and Constanza had eaten an early dinner before settling into the comforts of her pillows for a game show, the lingering fear that something else would end up being wrong had slowly ebbed away.

Unfortunately, it had left room for other emotions to creep in. Ugly emotions she couldn't seem to control. One minute she was furious at Damon for daring to question her, push her during one of the worst days of her life. The next she was livid with herself for losing control.

Beneath it all, heartbreak pounded so fiercely she could barely keep her tears at bay. When she'd seen Damon standing there, looking so handsome and commanding, she had wanted to run to him, to throw her arms around his neck and seek comfort and strength. She'd had to wrap her arms around her waist to keep herself from doing just that.

The more they'd talked, the angrier she'd become. As if breaking up with her hadn't been enough, he'd made his stance perfectly clear at the helipad when he'd held his hand out and shaken hers like they were nothing more than business associates. By not inviting her to be a part of the celebrations for the Royal Air contract. By not contacting her at all for nearly a month.

By doing what he always did and never letting her into his life.

And she'd accepted it. Yes, it had hurt, but she had respected his decision and stayed away, begun the slow and laborious process of rebuilding her life.

A process he had disrupted by reappearing at one of her most vulnerable points. Why had he bothered coming all the way uptown to the hospital? He'd reopened the wounds she'd worked so hard to close, kindled hopes that his presence meant something more than just concern. His offer to pay for Constanza's medical bills had infuriated her. She didn't want him to have any kind of presence in her life, any kind of impact. She wanted—*needed*—a clean break if she was going to survive this.

She closed her eyes as a particularly loud boom of thunder rattled the window. The stitches she'd spent so much time working on had been strained under the pain of his reappearance. They'd been ripped asunder by the words she'd hurled at him in anger.

Words she now deeply regretted. No matter how hurt she had been by his decisions, no matter how sad she had been by knowing he would never feel the same way about her as she felt about him, she had been deliberately cruel to the man she loved.

Lovers implies love. We didn't love each other.

"I can hear you thinking from here."

Evolet looked over her shoulder to see Constanza watching with an alertness she hadn't seen in a long time. She moved to the bedside and reached for a pillow.

"Fluff that pillow and I'll never make my hot chocolate for you again."

A small smile pulled at Evolet's lips. "Now that is a dire threat."

"Everyone keeps coming in to check my water, check the volume on the TV, fluff my pillows." Constanza huffed. "You can only fluff a pillow so many times. They're keeping an eye on me."

"It is a hospital, Constanza. And you did have a nasty fall."

Constanza's eyes softened.

"I fell. But I'm here." She reached over and grasped Evolet's hand. "I'm not going anywhere. Not yet."

A lump formed in Evolet's throat. "I was scared."

"I was, too." Her silver head dipped, her voice lowering. "I know sometimes I slip away. I know it happens more than I'd like. Every time I come back and realize I've forgotten for a while, it feels like I've lost another piece of myself." She looked up then and smiled, tears gathering in her eyes. "But then I see Samuel or I see you, and I take joy in those moments."

Evolet slowly sank down into a chair. She leaned forward and smoothed a curl back from Constanza's wrinkled face.

"How do you do it?" she asked. "How do you stay so strong?"

"I don't always. There are days when it's hard to get out of bed, moments when I come back from wherever I drift off to and I feel angry or confused or sad. But there's no guarantee that life will be perfect, child." Constanza cupped Evolet's cheek, her skin cool and dry, a balm against the heat of sorrow and anger. "In fact, it would be quite boring. I've told you of my life before I came here. So much loss, but so much joy, too. I am more resilient, and happier, because of the hardships I faced."

Half an hour later, after Constanza had fallen asleep, Evolet slipped downstairs and out into the night air, her adoptive mother's words of wisdom whirling inside her head. The thunderstorm still grumbled in the distance, but the rain had abated to a light mist that added a mystical air to the shops and restaurants that lined Madison Avenue. Golden light spilled out the windows of a bakery. A florist carried buckets overflowing with tulips and roses inside as he prepared to close for the night.

She sat on a bench under a blue awning. In the building behind her, babies were being born. People said their final goodbye to loved ones. Hope was given, and hope was taken away. In front of her, she watched people walk by, many clutching umbrellas, some sporting raincoats and a few braving the elements, dashing to and from jobs, dates, nights out with friends.

The world moved on. She needed to, too.

Even after she'd let Constanza into her heart, she'd kept it closed to everyone else. She'd told herself the temporary nature of her work gave her the flexibility to pursue her music career. That it had let her keep herself distant had been an added bonus. It had also served as an excuse to keep the members of the Apprentice Symphony at arm's length. She'd made progress over the past months, yes. But those had been baby steps, easing in without taking any true risks.

The one thing she had told herself she did without inhibition had been her music. But even that had been a lie. She had acquired the skills needed to play, yet she'd held herself back, hidden the passion she'd felt in the subway tunnels behind what she thought professional orchestras would want to hear.

She stood and moved to the edge of the awning. She watched the florist pick up another bucket, this one teeming with scarlet roses. A couple petals fell onto the sidewalk, bloodred against the rain-splattered gray concrete.

She'd hidden her passion for Damon, too. Oh, she'd loved him, had let herself feel more than she'd ever thought she would. But she hadn't told him. She'd kept it tucked safely away, a secret only she knew.

One step took her out into the rain. Soft drops felt cool on her exposed skin.

She hadn't even given him a chance. She'd waited for him to make a move, waited to see some confirmation that he might be feeling more. She had wanted all the joy, the pleasure that came from loving someone and none of the pain.

Perhaps, if she'd told Damon how she truly felt, he would've told her he didn't feel the same. Just the possibility of it left her shaken. But it would have been like the other moments she'd shared with Damon: her childhood, her music, the impact Constanza had had on her life. As she'd unburdened herself, the wounds she'd thought carved forever into her heart had begun to heal, enabling her to take those tiny steps that had already enriched her life so much. Whether Damon would have welcomed or returned her feelings was only part of it.

Still, she'd never given him the chance to tell her. And perhaps, in light of his coming down to the hospital today, there was a chance. A foundation, however small, they could build on to create something more. It might be a summer, a year, maybe longer. But she knew, with every fiber of her being, that she wanted to try.

She stepped back under the awning and pulled her phone out of her pocket. She would give him, and herself, a few days before she did anything rash like she'd done tonight.

She punched a number into her phone. There was one thing, though, that couldn't wait.

A male voice answered. She swallowed hard.

"Hi. This is Evolet Grey. I'm calling about my audition."

Damon stood in the middle of an empty warehouse-like building in Queens. Floors gleamed underfoot. Massive fan blades swirled in lazy circles. Newly installed lights lit up the space, including the upgraded bathrooms and employee breakrooms installed in the back. Offices had been added, including one for the plant foreman at the top of a flight of stairs with a bank of windows that would overlook the manufacturing of parts for Royal Air's luxury jets.

His tour had included designating a primary manufacturing site from one of Bradford Global's numerous properties. Come next Monday, it would be filled with contractors installing equipment, a team from human resources ready to oversee the massive hiring that needed to happen to stay on schedule, and cameras from the public relations department to document everything.

It was Bradford Global's biggest triumph in the history of the company. And Damon still felt empty. Gone was the pride that had previously filled his chest. The bone-deep satisfaction he usually experienced as he completed a tour of a facility before it started a project was absent.

All he could think about, standing inside the cavernous building, was that there was no one to share it with.

He walked across the floor, footsteps echoing off the soaring ceiling. For so long Bradford Global had been his family, his purpose. He controlled the outcomes, the successes and losses with what he invested in the company and in the people who worked for him. Any time he had felt that emotional tug, the subtle urge to get involved beyond the surface with someone, all he had to do was think back to the depths he'd sunk to in the weeks after his parents' deaths. The nights he'd drunk himself into a stupor, waking up on the floor of his bathroom while pain screamed through his head. The days he'd spent in the courthouse pews at the trial for his parents' killer, barely keeping his rage in check as he'd watched a scrawny kid with floppy hair sit behind the desk with his head bowed.

The grieving that had followed. The slow, painful journey to reigning himself back under control. The welcome relief of focusing on work, on throwing himself into working for his family's company and carrying on his father's legacy. The small allowances he'd made for himself to experience gratification with each achievement as Bradford Global had climbed higher and higher.

Alone had been safe. Alone had been his choice.

Now it was just lonely. Without someone to share with, without *Evolet*, he felt hollow. His fascination with her might have started with physical attraction. But it had so quickly bloomed into something more. Something he now knew, and accepted, as love.

He was thirty-three years old, and he was in love for the first time.

Slowly, he turned in a circle, imagining what it would be like to bring her here. She would pepper him with questions, want to know the how and the why and the when. He would soak up every moment, proud and happy knowing he had someone in his life who cared about the company, its people, its mission.

He'd hurt her. More than once. But he loved her. They had brought out the best in each other. He hadn't overcome everything he had in his life to give up now.

With determination twining through his veins, he pulled out his phone.

"Julie? I need you to do something for me."

CHAPTER NINETEEN

THE LANTERNS LINING the sidewalk cast a golden glow over trees flush with green leaves. Warmth lingered in the air, a pleasant heat that promised long nights, relaxation and the freedom that came with the onset of summer. People walked along Center Drive as it sloped up toward the bridge that overlooked the Central Park Carousel.

Evolet clutched the handle of her cello case tighter. It had been just shy of a week since Damon had done exactly as she'd asked and walked out of the hospital. A week that she hadn't heard from him. Not that she could blame him, she reminded herself sternly as she walked at a brisk pace past a playground. He'd done exactly as she'd asked. It was up to her to offer the olive branch.

Wednesday, she told herself firmly.

Her make-up audition was Tuesday. And then she would contact him.

Butterflies fluttered in her chest. She'd been torn on whether she should contact him sooner. But she had finally decided to wait until after the audition. She wanted to tell him that not only had he been right to challenge her but that she'd done it. Even if he told her he couldn't return her love, even if things were truly over, she wanted him to know the difference he'd made in her life.

Waiting had turned out to be a wise choice. The week had flown by. If she wasn't in Constanza's room playing, she was in the park or the Apprentice Symphony's practice room. She'd swallowed her nerves and reached out to Ashley and some of the other musicians, who had responded as if they'd been best friends for years and came to listen and critique her playing. More than once she'd turned away so they didn't see just how deeply moved she was by their support and burgeoning friendship.

She'd practiced the pieces on the audition list until concertos infiltrated her dreams. She hummed the melodies on the subway, the sidewalk, even in the grocery store until she'd seen a woman slowly sidle away from her in the produce aisle. No sooner had she decided that morning to take the day off than her phone had pinged with an email request from her website. A man named Charles was proposing at the Central Park Carousel and wanted her to play.

Her chest had tightened. Vivid memories had washed over her, standing so closely she'd felt the heat emanating from his body, soaked in his handsome profile lit up by the lanterns and carousel lights. Remembered how quickly her heart had pounded as an attraction she had never experienced nor expected had settled over her skin until her limbs had been heavy with the weight of her need.

She'd nearly ignored the email. But, she had decided after a few minutes of staring morosely into her tea, it was exactly the distraction she needed. The carousel had long been a source of enjoyment for her. Regardless of how things turned out with Damon, their walk that night had been an incredible moment in her life. One day, if she was fortunate enough to have a family of her own, she would take them to ride the carousel.

She wouldn't let the bleak moments take away her joy. Not anymore.

The carousel came into view. The lights were on, but the speakers that normally played the majestic music that accompanied the rise and fall of the horses were silent. No crowds of kids waiting excitedly outside the ticket booth, no parents armed with cameras.

Because of a barrier, she realized as she drew closer. Crowd-control barriers had been erected at the three sidewalk intersections that led to the carousel, with a security guard standing near each one. Signs hanging from the silver steel proclaimed: *Carousel closed for private event. Unlimited free rides to the public beginning at eight p.m.*

Her eyebrows shot up. The mysterious Charles had paid triple her normal fee, another incentive for her to accept the job, including a brief *Sorry for the late notice* note on his booking. Money was obviously no concern if he had rented the entire carousel for an hour and paid for the public to ride as much as they wanted the rest of the night.

She gave her name to one of the guards, who waved her through. She walked up to the carousel, her heels clicking against the pavement.

"Hello?"

"In here."

A muffled voice sounded from inside the carousel hall. She glanced around, taking some comfort in the presence of the security guards nearby, as she walked through the archway.

Her breath hitched as she drew closer to the carousel. She'd never gotten this close, always holding out for…something. Just another thing she had denied herself.

A chestnut-colored horse caught her eye. A bright orange saddle trimmed in reds and blues rested on its back. Its head was thrown back, the black mane shaped into wild spirals as if it were blowing in some imaginary breeze. She moved closer and laid a hand on the muzzle.

Tonight, she decided as she smiled. Tonight she would ride.

"Beautiful, isn't it?"

The tones of his voice, deep and smoky, rolled over her. She waited one moment, then two. Maybe she had just imagined it, manipulated someone else's voice in her head to sound like his.

Then she saw his reflection in the shiny wood that made up the horse's neck.

Slowly, she turned. He stood just a couple feet behind her, hands tucked casually into his pockets, his handsome face smooth and serene.

"What are you doing here?"

"Waiting for you."

"But where is…" Her mind fumbled, then latched on to a distant memory as they'd verbally sparred in his office. Her eyes narrowed. "Edward *Charles* Damon Bradford."

One corner of his mouth curved up as mischief glinted in his eyes. "I took a risk using Charles, but I didn't think you would remember."

"You could have called. Or texted." She glanced out the arch at the barricades and security guards. "You didn't have to go to all this trouble just to get me to talk to you."

His face sobered as his gaze sharpened. "The last time I saw you, you told me you didn't love me and to go away."

Heat flooded her face. She wanted to look down, away, anywhere but at the pain in his green eyes. But she didn't. She'd caused that pain, and she needed to take responsibility. "I did exactly what you accused me of. I used you as a punching bag that day. I'm sorry, Damon."

"I deserved it. And," he said as he took a slow but deliberate step closer, "I owe you an apology."

"For what?"

"The heliport. The way I let things end. Not opening up to you." His eyes rested on her face with sorrowful intensity. "Not letting you in because of my own pride and fear."

Her throat tightened as she remembered the coolness in his eyes, the efficiency of his handshake just hours after he'd seduced her with slow, drugging kisses.

"I set the terms of our arrangement, Damon. Yes, it hurt," she admitted, "but it was over. I knew not to expect more. If I did, that was on me."

"Don't do that," he whispered as he reached out and grabbed the cello case handle. His fingers brushed hers. The fleeting contact sizzled across her skin, and her lips parted on a sharp inhale. She let him take the case from her, set it down behind him.

When he took her hands in his, she swallowed hard. "Damon…"

"Five minutes, Evolet. Just five minutes to say what I need to. After that, if you still want me to go, I will."

She let him lead her to a chariot painted blue and trimmed in gold. He sat next to her and continued to hold her hands in his, his fingers stroking gently over her knuckles.

"I loved my parents."

He paused, his focus riveted on their hands. She waited, giving him time.

"It was easier for so long to just not talk about my parents. If I didn't talk about them, it wouldn't hurt. Sometimes I could even pretend they were just away on an extended vacation.

"I'm starting to realize how much of a disservice I'm doing to their memories, to what they did for me. There were sad ones, but there were good ones. So many good ones I'd just…banished." His voice faded as he turned to look at her. "It hurts to remember. But I think I'd rather hurt and remember than keep living without thinking of them from time to time." He leaned forward, forearms resting on his knees, hands clenched together. "My mom would make me breakfast every morning before she went to the hospital. She worked as a nurse delivering babies. Most days were happy, but sometimes she would come home sad. She felt every joy, every loss like it was her own, and her patients loved her for it. Even after Bradford Global grew, she kept her job."

His fingers tightened around hers.

"My dad…my earliest memory is walking through one of our factories with him holding my hand. He took me everywhere, told me if I wanted to be a part of Bradford Global I could but I'd have to earn it. He told me…a week before he died…that I had surpassed all of his expectations. That he was proud of me."

He grated the last words out before he bowed his head. She didn't offer empty words of comfort or push him for more. She just wrapped her arms around his neck and held him close. He buried his face in her hair and breathed in.

"They were driving home from a date. Married twenty-three years and they still went on a date every week like they were teenagers. It wasn't even nine o'clock at night, and some drunk college bastard was driving eighty miles an hour through their neighborhood."

Evolet's hold on him tightened.

"I loved them. I loved them, and then they were gone. It was just the three of us for so long. I had friends, of course, girlfriends in high school and college. But my parents… I loved them deeply. When I lost them, I lost myself for a long time. At first I could barely get out of bed. Getting out of bed meant having to face an empty house, walk past their rooms and know they were never coming back. I had nightmares. I drank too much. I couldn't control my grief.

"And then I got angry. I'd never felt so much anger.

"I attended the trial for the driver who killed them. When the judge announced he would get the maximum sentence for what he'd been charged with, fifteen years in prison, I almost smiled. I felt…happy. Happy that he was being punished. A pale comparison to the price my parents had paid, but at least some justice had been done."

She gently lifted one hand to his cheek. He turned his head into her caress, pressed a kiss to her palm.

"And then I saw the same skinny kid turn to look at his parents and burst into tears. I watched as his father held him, his mother kissed him. They walked up to me as their son was taken away in shackles and told me they were sorry for what their boy did. The woman handed me a sympathy card. Her hands were shaking."

Evolet's heart broke for all the losses suffered. But most of all for the man just out of boyhood who had lost the people he loved the most.

"I sat in the courthouse long after they'd left, holding the card, and grieved. My parents lost their lives. Two other parents had theirs forever changed. And while that boy will have some time when he gets out, he lost so much because of one selfish, stupid decision."

He looked up at her then, his eyes fierce. "I lost myself in my emotions during those months. One moment I was filled with hate and rage, the next I felt like I was drowning."

With her heart in her throat, she slowly slipped her arms around his waist. He let his head drop, rested his forehead against hers as he pulled her closer until she held tight against him, their breaths mingling in the summer air.

"After I walked out of the courthouse, I swore I would never let myself feel like that again. I twisted it in my head that loving someone as deeply as I loved my parents was opening the door to how I felt in those months after I lost them. And once I saw how that boy's parents were affected, saw him cry and turn to his mother for comfort, I felt the hate drain out of me. It left me feeling empty."

He pulled back, caught her chin in his hand.

"Empty was easy. Empty meant not opening myself

to get lost again, to be so hurt. And for a long time that worked. Until you, Evolet."

A tremble passed through her as she realized the emotion in his eyes had changed from sorrow to something bright. Something that made hope bloom in her chest. Once she would have squashed it, pulled back rather than risk getting hurt.

But not anymore.

"It took me too long to figure out what I felt for you." He stood, bringing her with him, her body molding to his. "Some part of me knew that day at the hell port, told me I was an idiot for letting you walk away. I was too damned scared to admit that I had fallen in love with you, Evolet."

She surged forward, throwing her arms around his neck and kissing him with a wild abandon that just weeks ago she wouldn't have let herself surrender to. Damon groaned and held her so tightly it was a wonder they didn't melt into each other.

"Damon," she whispered between kisses, "I lied." He started to jerk back, but her fingers slipped into his hair and kept him close. "I love you, too."

He laughed, uninhibited and deep and joyful. "I missed you."

The simple words brought tears to her eyes. "I missed you. I was going to call you on Wednesday after my audition—"

"Your audition?" A smile spread across his face. "You called them."

"You were right." She brushed at her eyes. "I knew I was in love you, but I alternated between hoping you would say something first or telling myself it would never go beyond our arrangement, so why bother. It made me realize how long I've been holding pieces of myself back, even from my music. So I called, and I audition on Tuesday. I wanted to wait until I went, until I did it, so I could tell you that I love you and that you were right and that even if I didn't get it I tried and—"

He cut off her babbling with another kiss that thrilled her all the way to her toes. "I'm proud of you, Evolet."

She did cry then, happy tears that slid down her cheeks as he stood and swept her up into his arms.

"Which horse do you want to ride?"

She pointed to the horse that had first caught her eye. He carried her over and set her on its back.

"Aren't you going to join me?"

"Yes. I'm looking forward to being your first. Again," he added with a wicked grin that sent a bolt of electricity careening through her. "But first things first. When I booked your services, I asked for you to be present for a proposal."

Blood roared in her ears as he reached into his back pocket and pulled out a small black box. Her breath caught as he flipped the lid to reveal a silver band with a glittering amber-colored jewel.

"When I saw this stone, citrine, it reminded me of your eyes."

Her tears began to fall harder. "Damon…"

"Marry me, Evolet. I don't want to go another day without you in my life."

She framed his face in her hands and poured every ounce of love she felt into her kiss. "Yes, Damon. Yes."

He slipped the ring onto her finger, a perfect fit.

"One moment."

He jogged over to the wall, pressed a button and then

came back over as the carousel sprung to life. Music filtered out as the horse rose up. Damon placed his foot in the stirrup and swung himself up behind her, pulling her snug against his chest.

"I think it's one rider per horse," she teased.

"Are you complaining?"

She felt him grow hard against her back and pressed against him, savored his groan. "Not if you're going to take me somewhere after to seduce me."

"Didn't I mention that was part of you agreeing to marry me?"

She laughed and leaned back into his embrace. The carousel spun, horses rising and falling, music playing, the jewel of her ring glimmering beneath the lights.

"Damon."

"Yes?"

"I love you."

He pressed a tender kiss to her cheek.

"And I love you, Evolet." She felt his smile. "We're going to have a wonderful life together."

EPILOGUE

Seven years later

CHARLES BRADFORD LOOKED up at his father, a crease between his barely there eyebrows, as a horrific screeching filled the air.

"I agree, son," Damon said with a wince. "Your sister needs more practice."

Footsteps sounded on the stairs. Evolet walked down, a forced smile on her face as she glanced over her shoulder. Seven years of being married hadn't stopped Damon's breath from catching when he saw his wife. Her hair fell shorter these days, easier to manage as a mom of two and a professional cellist with the Emerald City Philharmonic.

"Yes, honey. It does sound a little better." She shot Damon a hot look as he chuckled. "She's holding the bow better than she did last week."

"Too bad she's not playing better than she did last week," he said with an affectionate glance up at the ceiling. Rashael Bradford was proving to be a very determined, though not talented, cello player.

Evolet started to protest, then sank down into a chair

next to Charlie's highchair with a grin and kissed his chubby cheek. "Not even the slightest."

Charlie babbled at his mother before resuming his destruction of the eggs on his plate. Wisps of blond hair had finally started to cover his bald head. Between his gummy smiles and big green eyes, Damon was besotted with his son.

As besotted as he'd been when he'd held his daughter in his arms for the first time four years ago and realized he could fall in love more than once in a lifetime.

"Don't take it too hard, darling." Damon moved to his wife, tilted her chin up and kissed her. "Not everyone can be a child prodigy."

She smiled against his mouth. His body stirred.

"When does Charlie go down for his nap?"

Evolet glanced at the clock and groaned. "Not until eleven."

"And where will Rashael be at eleven a.m.?"

"With Samuel, Sarah and Constanza at the park."

Damon's wedding gift to Evolet had been converting part of his penthouse into a small apartment for Constanza. Having Constanza join them in the mornings for breakfast, relaxing on the terrace or, most importantly, spending time with her grandchildren had not only made Evolet and Constanza happy, it had also given Damon another taste of having a maternal figure in his life. Getting to know Constanza's son, Samuel, and, as of five years ago, his new wife, Sarah, had added more faces around the table for Sunday dinners and holidays.

It wasn't always easy. He and Evolet had both noticed Constanza struggling a little more with losing track of time or fumbling with names. The disease had progressed and would continue to do so. But he also knew that he and Evolet would be there for Constanza to help her navigate the changes in her life.

Just as they would be there for each other, for the good times and the bad.

Damon rubbed his hands up and down Evolet's arms. "So, what I'm hearing is we have an empty penthouse, a sunny day and a beautiful pool."

"Why Mr. Bradford, are you proposing playing hooky from work?"

"I think I'm overdue for some time off."

The Royal Air contract had been the beginning of a massive expansion of Bradford Global. When they had delivered the planes not only on time but under budget, business had skyrocketed with requests coming in from around the world. New plants were going up every year. Offices had expanded.

And Damon had hired more administrators to share duties with. Bradford Global still held an important place in his life and always would.

But, he thought as Evolet's arms twined around his neck, *not the most important*.

He was leaning down to kiss his wife again when another blast of music echoed down the stairs.

"Any chance we could get her to switch over to the drums?"

"I'm not sure which would be worse. She still insists she's ready to play in the concert at her preschool tomorrow." Her nose scrunched as Rashael's cello let out another indignant squawk from above. "What do I do?"

"Let her. She'll have fun. Next week she'll be on to something else."

She smiled, then reached up and framed his face

with her hands. "Have I told you lately that I love you very much?"

"I believe you said something about it this morning when you woke me up."

"Uh, I believe it was you who woke me up when you slipped my nightgown off," Evolet replied as her hands slipped down over his neck, her fingertips grazing his skin. "Not that I minded—"

"Mommy!"

Rashael hopped down the stairs, her round face framed by dark waves of hair, her golden-brown eyes round with excitement. "I'm ready for the concert!"

Evolet grazed Damon's lips with her own once more before moving over to the stairs to sweep their daughter into her arms. "I can't wait to see you play, baby."

"And we get to go to the carousel afterward, right?"

"Absolutely."

Damon leaned against the kitchen counter, his eyes flickering between his wife, his daughter and his son. Evolet looked up at him, love shining in her eyes.

"What are you thinking?" she asked softly.

"That I was right."

"Oh?"

"Yeah." He pulled her into his arms against the backdrop of Rashael's delighted squeal. "We have a wonderful life."

* * * * *

#4153 THE MAID'S PREGNANCY BOMBSHELL
Cinderella Sisters for Billionaires
by Lynne Graham
Shy hotel maid Alana is so desperate to clear a family debt that when she discovers Greek tycoon Ares urgently needs a wife, she blurts out a scandalous suggestion: she'll become his convenient bride. But as chemistry blazes between them, she has an announcement that will inconveniently disrupt his well-ordered world. She's having his baby!

#4154 A BILLION-DOLLAR HEIR FOR CHRISTMAS
by Caitlin Crews
When Tiago Villela discovers Lillie Merton is expecting, a wedding is nonnegotiable. To protect the Villela billions, his child must be legitimate. But his plan for a purely pragmatic arrangement is soon threatened by a dangerously insatiable desire...

#4155 A CHRISTMAS CONSEQUENCE FOR THE GREEK
Heirs to a Greek Empire
by Lucy King
Booking billionaire Zander's birthday is a triumph for caterer Mia. And the hottest thing on the menu? A scorching one-night stand! But a month later, he can't be reached. Mia finally ambushes him at work to reveal she's pregnant! He insists she move in with him, but this Christmas she wants all or nothing!

#4156 MISTAKEN AS HIS ROYAL BRIDE
Princess Brides for Royal Brothers
by Abby Green
Maddi hadn't fully considered the implications of posing as her secret half sister. *Or* that King Aristedes would demand she continue the pretense as his intended bride. Immersing herself in the royal life she was denied growing up is as compelling as it is daunting. But so is the thrill of Aristedes's smoldering gaze...

HPCNMRA1023

#4157 VIRGIN'S STOLEN NIGHTS WITH THE BOSS
Heirs to the Romero Empire
by Carol Marinelli
Polo player Elias rarely spares a glance for his staff, until he meets stable hand and former heiress Carmen. And their attraction is irresistible! Elias knows he'll give the innocent all the pleasure she could want, but that's it. Unless their passion can unlock a connection much harder to walk away from...

#4158 CROWNED FOR THE KING'S SECRET
Behind the Palace Doors...
by Kali Anthony
One year ago, her spine-tingling night with exiled king Sandro left Victoria pregnant and alone. Lied to by the palace, she believed he wanted nothing to do with them. So Sandro turning up on her doorstep—ready to claim her, his heir and his kingdom—is astounding!

#4159 HIS INNOCENT UNWRAPPED IN ICELAND
by Jackie Ashenden
Orion North wants Isla's company...and her! So when the opportunity to claim both at the convenient altar arises, he takes it. But with tragedy in his past, even their passion may not be enough to melt the ice encasing his heart...

#4160 THE CONVENIENT COSENTINO WIFE
by Jane Porter
Clare Redmond retreated from the world, pregnant and grieving her fiancé's death, never expecting to see his ice-cold brother, Rocco, again. She's stunned when the man who always avoided her storms back into her life, demanding they wed to give her son the life a Cosentino deserves!

YOU CAN FIND MORE INFORMATION ON UPCOMING HARLEQUIN TITLES, FREE EXCERPTS AND MORE AT HARLEQUIN.COM.

HPCNMRB1023

Get 3 FREE REWARDS!

We'll send you 2 FREE Books plus a FREE Mystery Gift.

FREE
Value Over
$20

Both the **Harlequin® Desire** and **Harlequin Presents®** series feature compelling novels filled with passion, sensuality and intriguing scandals.

YES! Please send me 2 FREE novels from the Harlequin Desire or Harlequin Presents series and my FREE gift (gift is worth about $10 retail). After receiving them, if I don't wish to receive any more books, I can return the shipping statement marked "cancel." If I don't cancel, I will receive 6 brand-new Harlequin Presents Larger-Print books every month and be billed just $6.30 each in the U.S. or $6.49 each in Canada, a savings of at least 10% off the cover price, or 3 Harlequin Desire books (2-in-1 story editions) every month and be billed just $7.83 each in the U.S. or $8.43 each in Canada, a savings of at least 12% off the cover price. It's quite a bargain! Shipping and handling is just 50¢ per book in the U.S. and $1.25 per book in Canada.* I understand that accepting the 2 free books and gift places me under no obligation to buy anything. I can always return a shipment and cancel at any time by calling the number below. The free books and gift are mine to keep no matter what I decide.

Choose one. ☐ **Harlequin Desire**
(225/326 BPA GRNA)

☐ **Harlequin Presents Larger-Print**
(176/376 BPA GRNA)

☐ **Or Try Both!**
(225/326 & 176/376 BPA GRQP)

Name (please print)

Address — Apt. #

City — State/Province — Zip/Postal Code

Email: Please check this box ☐ if you would like to receive newsletters and promotional emails from Harlequin Enterprises ULC and its affiliates. You can unsubscribe anytime.

Mail to the Harlequin Reader Service:
IN U.S.A.: P.O. Box 1341, Buffalo, NY 14240-8531
IN CANADA: P.O. Box 603, Fort Erie, Ontario L2A 5X3

Want to try 2 free books from another series! Call 1-800-873-8635 or visit www.ReaderService.com.

HARLEQUIN
PLUS

Try the best multimedia
subscription service for romance
readers like you!

Read, Watch and Play.

Experience the easiest way to get
the romance content you crave.

Start your **FREE TRIAL** at
<u>www.harlequinplus.com/freetrial</u>.